59

STRANGERS IN THE NIGHT

The man of her dreams sweeps Dee into a romantic last dance at her friend's wedding — then promptly disappears. When they meet again, it's in unpleasant circumstances. She finds that they are on opposite sides in a conflict that involves a promise Dee made to her favourite aunt. There is no way to resolve the situation — Dee cannot compromise, yet her heart tells her that Jack is the man for her. Sometimes however, love will find a way . . .

BETH JAMES

STRANGERS IN THE NIGHT

Complete and Unabridged

LINFORD
Leicester

First published in Great Britain in 2009

First Linford Edition
published 2011

British Library CIP Data

James, Beth.
    Strangers in the night. - -
    (Linford romance library)
    1. Love stories.
    2. Large type books.
    I. Title II. Series
    823.9′2–dc22

    ISBN 978–1–4448–0689–2

Published by
F. A. Thorpe (Publishing)
Anstey, Leicestershire

Set by Words & Graphics Ltd.
Anstey, Leicestershire
Printed and bound in Great Britain by
T. J. International Ltd., Padstow, Cornwall

This book is printed on acid-free paper

1

Oh, no! Albeit subtly, the already dim lighting was being subdued even further and as the first well known bars of a romantic song about a lady in red sounded, the bride and groom took to the floor for the last dance.

Dee Stanley leaned against the wall, hoping she would merge with the shadows and pass for a fold of decorative drapery or a large indoor plant. Anything really, other than being recognised as the wallflower she undoubtedly was.

In the middle distance she could only just about make out the white blur that was her childhood friend, Gina's wedding dress, hopefully with Gina inside it, and the dark suit next to the white mass which must be John, Gina's new husband.

Ah well, at least being short sighted,

and without either her contact lenses or glasses, meant that she couldn't see any expressions of pity on the other guests faces, as they realised her own solitary state.

Was there anything worse than attending a wedding on your own? Being a lone bystander through the greetings, eatings, drinkings, not to mention the photos, flowers, speeches and face stretching smiling. But you'd do it for a friend. And Gina had been a good friend of Dee's since their early childhood.

Even though they'd been separated at the time of Dee's parents move up to Surrey when she was only twelve, the friendship had endured through letters and phone calls. And now fifteen years later, when Gina asked Dee to be one of her four bridesmaids, Dee hadn't had the heart to refuse.

Determinedly, she fixed a half smile on her lips. She would not feel sorry for herself. Why should she? Hadn't she just landed herself a job she knew she would love, located back in the area where she had grown up? Not only that, but now she would be able to visit her favourite Great Aunt Louisa on a regular basis.

Only a year ago, due to a bad heart condition, Aunt Louisa had sold Brook House, her old childhood home, and taken up residence in Stafford Place, a luxurious old people's home.

Always gregarious, Louisa settled in well and never complained but Dee knew she missed the old house, which contained so many of her childhood memories. Yes, Dee would be very happy to spend more time with Aunt Louisa. All in all, she was looking forward to the future; the chance to once more catch up with old school friends, and to make a new life for herself away from Ray.

Only she wasn't going to think about Ray now, was she? Ray with the swift smile and the equally swift memory, so it would seem. Ray with the sunny disposition, with the charming repartee, the American accent, and oh yes, the American wife, he'd forgotten to mention.

Dee didn't need to convince herself she'd done the right thing in deciding to leave him in London and scurry back to the place she's always thought of as home. But naturally, her friends had moved on with their lives and, while they were welcoming when they heard of her return, there couldn't help but be large gaps in their histories which might sometimes make Dee feel an outsider.

But here she was at the close of Gina's wedding. The guests had been friendly and her bridesmaidly duties, which included socialising and ensuring everyone knew their way round the large leisure complex where the reception, one of several, was being held were nearly at an end. And she'd enjoyed it; she really had — up until now.

Up to the last dance.

Dee stood there in her dress of deep old rose, examining her half full glass as though it was the most fascinating object she'd ever seen.

'Dance with me!'

Dee's head snapped up with surprise. There in front of her stood the most drop dead gorgeous man she'd ever set her short sighted eyes on. Well, she thought he was probably drop dead gorgeous because, given the circumstances, anyone a shade more handsome than Quasimodo would have to appeal. She could just about make him out in the half light.

Dark hair, beaky nose. Tall and muscular. Well, that would do for starters. He was wearing a white shirt and a loosened tie and had a rose in the buttonhole of his dark suit jacket.

'Well?' It was a question this time rather than a statement. Hurriedly, Dee slid her drink on to the nearest table. She loved to dance. What on earth was she doing opening and shutting her mouth like a goldfish?

'I'd love to,' she said, moving into his arms.

Afterwards she thought she must have dreamt it. The tender strands of music wrapping round her, his strong arms holding her, the warmth of his chest radiating through his cotton shirt and her heart beating hard next to it. Perhaps she imagined the waves of desire; the strange trembling that had possessed her as they turned slowly, caught in the magic of the song. It was as though they were the only two people alive and the rest just extras in their performance.

They didn't speak. The handsome stranger didn't seem to feel the need and, as she dealt with all the other sensations pulsating through her body, Dee found the power of speech had deserted her.

His hand was dry and cool on her back. The fragrance of his aftershave lingered, tangy, in her nostrils. Somehow her body fitted with his easily and naturally, and something in her soul was telling her that this was right, this was how it was meant to be.

It was ridiculous, she thought next morning. Utterly mad. People didn't meet and fall in love during one dance and no conversation. Especially not people like her, a sensible twenty-seven-year-old, junior school teacher.

Sensible — who's sensible? the other half of her argued. Sensible people, who were as blind as a bat, didn't go to weddings without their glasses when their contact lenses have grown a strange fungal disease.

Sensible people would take their glasses, disguised by their bouquet of flowers if necessary, and wear them once the ceremony was over. Then at least, they might stand a chance of recognising Prince Charming should they ever set eyes on him again.

Angrily she shook herself. He was probably another Ray, married with six children. No, that was an exaggeration, Ray had only had one child. Not that that made any difference.

The fact that he'd had a wife, and lied about it, and that she'd been stupid enough to believe him, surely that should be enough to put her off men for life.

Anyway, PC (Prince Charming) probably only took pity on a poor partnerless girl crying into her wine glass and just danced with her out of charity. Dee winced. No, she couldn't bear to be the object of pity, she'd rather think of him as a rat of the two-legged variety, out just for what he could get.

Only he hadn't asked for anything had he? Not a telephone number, not a name or an address, or even that of a friend in common. Not even a kiss come to that. Shame, a kiss might have been nice. Probably would have been heaven in fact.

Dee shivered, remembering the way he'd bent his head, looked into her eyes, drawn a long shuddering breath of . . . what? Desire? Horror? Indigestion? A rueful smile tugged at her lips as she admitted she didn't know. She'd just briefly shut her eyes anticipating . . . what? A kiss? A proposal?

Oh come on; get real, she told herself again. Things like that don't happen. Didn't happen, because when she'd opened her eyes again — he'd gone.

Vanished on the stroke of twelve just like Cinderella. Only she was Cinderella surely? And he should have been Prince Charming . . .

But wasn't — obviously!

'Who was he?'

'Well, it was your wedding, surely you should know.'

It was three weeks later and Gina and Dee sat facing each other in their favourite coffee bar with a cappuccino and a latte steaming on the table between them.

'Thing is, I don't.' Gina screwed up her forehead as she flicked through the photos on her digital camera. 'Thing is, although my sister's never been much good as a photographer, I did ask her to take a photo of every guest and she's very reliable at things like that. Just like you're reliable at organising people and getting them to the right table at the right time, making sure they don't drink too much or start a fight or anything.'

'Thanks a lot,' said Dee. 'You make me sound like a cross between a prison warden and a children's entertainer.'

'Precisely . . . The ideal bridesmaid.' Gina passed the camera back across the table. 'Are you sure he's not on here?'

'Positive.' Dee kept her voice light. Ridiculous to feel so disappointed, stupid to have been so sure she would be able to track PC (Prince Charming) down so easily. Anyway, what if she did find out who he was, what would she do then? Start following him or something? Get herself arrested as a stalker?

Yes, that would be a good way to start a new job. She could visualise the headlines already: *Deirdre Stanley — Manhunting Stalker — Would You Want Your Child Taught By This Woman?*

'It really doesn't matter. Couldn't matter less.'

'Well, it does though. I mean a strange bloke has turned up at my wedding. According to you he's on none of the photos, I've described him to John, well — the very sketchy description you gave me — and he can't think who he could be. We went through the list of evening only guests and we've identified them all on the photos — it's just such a mystery.'

For a moment, the two girls stared at one another.

'No, I didn't make him up,' said Dee in answer to the unspoken question in Gina's eyes. 'I know I'm a bit strange at times, but I haven't moved into fantasy land yet.'

'Of course you didn't make him up — I know that.' But the expression on Gina's face still said that she wasn't quite sure. 'It's just well, so odd!'

'It's no big deal. I was just curious, that's all. To tell the truth, the whole thing was a bit of a blur, you know, what with my lenses being infected with the lurgi and not having my specs, it's a wonder I saw anything at all that wasn't within a half metre radius. I'm just grateful I didn't miss my mouth with my food and managed to direct the wine into my glass OK, you know how I hate to waste a good wine.'

Halfway to taking a sip of her coffee, Gina suddenly smacked her hand to her head.

'Whoops! Calm down Gina, you nearly had coffee all over me and this my very favourite T-shirt by the way.'

Gina flapped her hands in the air. 'I've got it, I've got it . . . Of course.'

'What?'

'He must have been a waiter,' said Gina triumphantly. 'I mean it's obvious. It's the end of the evening, the lights are low. Everything's been cleared away. They're all just standing around waiting for the guests to go. And then . . . '

'And then?'

'And then they play his favourite song, and there across a crowded room, he sees a lady in red . . . '

'Old rose,' interrupted Dee.

'Near enough to make no difference . . . He sees you. The woman of his dreams. Dark hair curling gently on to her cheek. Eyelashes downcast, modestly blushing, and oh joy, alone. Can this be true? he asks himself. Then — this is my chance to dance with this divine creature. He crosses to her side . . .'

Dee blinked a few times. 'Sorry to upset you, but he wasn't a waiter.'

Gina looked crestfallen. 'How can you be so sure?'

'Wrong clothes, wrong manner. Not a waiter, I know he wasn't . . . Now let's talk about something else. How were the Italian Lakes?'

'Blue and wet. He didn't leave a shoe behind, did he?'

'Oh, give it a rest. I had one dance with him. It's a mystery, but not one I'm going to lose any sleep over I can assure you.'

'OK,' said Gina. 'But it was you who said it was a bit like Cinderella in reverse.'

'Hmm, well, I was exaggerating. I'm not going to give him another thought.'

'Yes, I can quite see that,' answered Gina with heavy irony.

★   ★   ★

Jack Lumsden smoothed a hand over his spiky hair, which spiked straight up again. He had a pile of folders on the desk in front of him and he still hadn't gone through them.

Well, that wasn't strictly true. He had tried to go through them. He'd sat staring at the specifications of the buildings, he'd attempted a little wild mathematics in a brain which felt as though it were made of cotton wool and he'd drunk two cups of coffee. But even he couldn't fool himself that the last half hour had been productive.

Restlessly, he pushed his chair back and took a turn round the cramped but tidy office. He felt like a caged lion, he knew he needed to get out, to be doing something constructive.

He should get in his car and go and inspect some proposed sites, call in at the auction rooms and find out if anything good was in the offing. Get cracking, get on a roll, get productive.

Jack picked up his keys and swung down the stairs. Yep, this was better.

Just keep moving, don't think about this morning, and certainly don't let your memory drag you back to three weeks, one day, and several hours ago. Stop living in la la land. Get a grip and get on with your life Jack. Get on with what you're good at. Get on with what's important. Get on with making money.

Several minutes later he realised, that instead of heading north as he'd intended towards a half developed site with a drainage problem, he was travelling in a southerly direction on the reverse route to the one he'd taken earlier that morning. The route where suddenly, like a punch in the solar plexus he'd caught a glimpse of her again.

Angrily, Jack glanced in his rear view mirror and changed lanes. At the next roundabout he'd head back north. There was no way any rational person could let a chance, less than five minutes, encounter rule them this way.

But this morning, 'the glimpse', had got him.

She was sitting stationary, at traffic lights. The fingers of one elegant hand were drumming on the steering wheel of her car and her eyes were fixed ahead of her, giving Jack a perfect view of her perfect profile. Her shining dark hair curved near the hollow of her soft cheek. And the line where her jawbone joined her throat was so delicate Jack wanted to reach out through his window and hers, and stroke it.

How could she sit there oblivious to his silent paralysis, less than three feet away? How could he sit there with his foot still on the clutch without shouting for her to stop, look his way, run away with him — without looking back?

Yes, it had given him a jolt. Actually, more than a jolt. More like an electric shock of the near fatal variety. He'd continued his journey to his office on auto-pilot, then wasted half an hour staring at the folders with only half of his mind functioning. And now here he was, driving in the wrong direction, reliving that fateful evening.

The evening where he'd done a single impetuous thing which, it seemed, had led to him taking leave of his senses.

It had been such a near miss. Jack really hadn't intended to put in an appearance at his uncle's wedding. For one thing, he hated weddings, and for another thing he had work to do and with Jack work was always a priority. In the end though he'd gone, in order to please his sister more than anything. So much for trying to do the right thing.

The wedding had been boring in its predictability, and he'd hated being on his own. Well, not on his own precisely, but partnerless, which was always something that made itself felt at a wedding.

Any other function and it didn't matter, but a wedding, well. Jack could almost see all the old aunties putting their heads together and whispering about Jack, all on his own again, what a shame that he couldn't meet a nice girl and settle down. Jack had smiled until his face felt as though it was frozen in a force nine snowstorm, then taken refuge in a bottle of rather fine red.

The venue had been interesting. One of these old houses that had started life as a rather modest manor house in Tudor times and had wings added and demolished according to the fluctuating fortunes of the family. Not many families owned homes like these anymore and, true to form, this one had been redeveloped into a hotel and leisure centre. Through Jack's eyes it looked to be a decent, fairly sympathetic, conversion. He wished he'd been involved in its regeneration.

He knew that despite his lack of orthodox qualifications, he had an eye for development and an empathy for buildings. As the evening wore on he decided to take a poke around. He was rather intrigued to know, for example, the size of the other function room across the large beamed hall.

And that was the trouble. Born to be curious, Jack had crossed to the next door, so to speak, wedding, lounged in the doorway and seen her.

She was holding a glass. Looking into it in a way that Jack immediately recognised as an *I wish I was anywhere else other than here* fashion. Then, even as he watched, he saw her look up, straighten her shoulders and fix a smile of enjoyment on to her face.

Before Jack had registered what he was about to do, he'd crossed the floor to be by her side. And when he'd got there, he realised how sweet she looked. Sweet and vulnerable. Enough to take his breath away.

He couldn't remember now, what he'd said. Something quite abrupt like, 'Please dance with me.' Or he might not have been as polite as that.

Whatever he'd said, she'd looked up, stared at him with the eyes of a startled fawn, not that he recalled ever having seen a fawn, startled or otherwise, but the next thing he knew she was in his arms and his heart.

No! He simply wasn't going to go there. Jack Lumsden had a five year

19

plan and girls, other than ones chosen as friends only, were not part of that plan. Maybe later when he was thirty-seven, say, yes, thirty-seven sounded like a good sort of age to settle down. Maybe if she, with the dark hair and fawn like eyes, crossed his path again he'd feel more ready to get to know her better, explore the possibilities. But not now. Not Jack.

She must live in the area, he deduced, five futile minutes of trying to put her out of his mind, later. He might even bump into her again. It was possible that he'd draw up at the same set of traffic lights at the same time of morning, glance casually across and meet her eyes. And then what?

Before he knew it, his minimalist flat would be full of cushions and soft cuddly toys, he'd be expected to phone her or text her every five minutes, he'd be nothing short of a slave. A slave to . . . Jack caught himself up on the word 'love'. The word 'love' was forbidden in Jack's brain, because he knew that love didn't exist. Especially love of the 'eyes meeting across a crowded room' nature.

So forget her, Jack. Forget how sweet she felt in your arms, how she smelled and how her head just nestled beneath your chin as though it were just made to fit there. Forget romance. Forget her.

2

Well, it was good in a way, thought Dee to herself as she headed out of town to pick up Aunt Louisa, good that Gina hadn't a clue who PC was. It was much better this way because now she could put him out of her mind once and for all and not keep thinking that maybe she'd bump into him in the library for example, which was extremely unlikely.

Being a school teacher, and an avid reader besides, Dee was a great library fan, but had to admit that library users were mainly in the region of five years old or fifty, with not too many in between. Anyway what was she doing thinking about libraries when she wouldn't be using one in this area until she moved down here permanently at the beginning of the summer holidays?

With a scrunch of gravel she drew up in the car park of Stafford Place, the residential home where Aunt Louisa now lived. This would be the last time she would be visiting until she came down to Dawlish for good. The thought was a good one. It had been a long journey to make every couple of months just for a weekend. Hopefully with a cheaper flat to pay rent on she might soon be able to afford to buy her own flat not too long after she took up her new teaching post just outside Dawlish.

Aunt Louisa was as welcoming as ever. 'Hello darling, what a lovely surprise. You were only here three weeks ago.'

'I know. It's only a flying visit. Stayed overnight at Gina's and picked up some bits I'd left at her place when I came for the wedding. The good news is though, I've found a flat for rent quite near here and I can move in as soon as term ends.'

Aunt Louisa's faded brown eyes crinkled at the corners. 'That's wonderful. I must say when I watch the news sometimes I do worry about you living up in London, such terrible things seem to happen. I think you're very wise to come back to Devon.'

'Well, Mum and Dad have got used to the idea now as well. Particularly Dad, he's always looking for an excuse to come back to these parts and visit his favourite aunt. Speaking of which, is my favourite aunt ready for a quick drive out for some lunch before I head back to dirty old London for the rest of the term?'

It was a warm day, but oppressive clouds were hanging low in the sky. Although Louisa was small, she was quite frail and walking made her breathless. It took quite some time to get her settled into Dee's car.

Once comfortable Louisa wanted to know all about Dee's new appointment at a local junior school.

'Oh, I know I'm going to love it,' enthused Dee. 'It's a lovely school. They don't have a fast turnover of staff, always a good sign, and I'm taking the seven to eight-year-olds, and they're always so sweet and anxious when they first go up to the big school. I'm really looking forward to it.'

Then Louisa wanted to know all about Gina's wedding. 'Did you meet anyone interesting there?' she asked with casual interest once the topics of the bride's dress, the weather, the bridesmaids and the funny speeches were exhausted.

'You're about as subtle as Mum,' answered Dee: 'I'll tell you the same as I told her. I'm not in the market for a new relationship. I just want to get my life sorted out and concentrate on having a bit of fun with no strings attached, for a change . . . There was a moment though,' she added. Then she gave a laugh. 'Too PC for words.'

'Politically Correct, you mean?'

Dee laughed. 'No, PC as in Prince Charming. I had one dance with him, he disappeared on the stroke of midnight and nobody knows where he came from or who he was.'

'Did he leave a shoe behind?'

'That's what Gina said . . . Unfortunately not! Just an air of mystery.'

They chatted amicably on for the remainder of the short drive to Louisa's favourite pub-come-restaurant, or rather Dee chatted and Louisa, eyes sparkling, listened.

'I don't know where you get your energy from,' she commented when at last there was a lull in the conversation. 'You're always so full of life, so ready to embrace the next experience.' A small sigh escaped her. 'It must be so nice to be young!'

Dee gave her a sideways glance. 'Sorry, I've been rabbiting on a bit . . . It's a habit of mine I'm afraid. How're things at Stafford Place?'

'Oh I can't complain. The staff are wonderful, the food is good, I know really I'm a very lucky woman. It's just that sometimes I feel maybe I was a little precipitate in selling Brook House and coming here. I'm sure I could have managed on my own a little longer.'

'Aunt Louisa, just think a moment. I know you loved the house, I did too, but as you said to me at the time, things change, life moves on. It was cold there in the winter, and it needed constant attention . . . You were advised by the doctor that you had years ahead of you if you'd only take it easy . . . ' Dee paused and shot another sidelong glance at her aunt. 'You are happy at Stafford Place aren't you?'

Louisa smiled. 'Yes, of course I am and you're quite right the house was getting too much for me. I'm just a stubborn old woman. Far better to have sold it to someone I like, who I know won't modernise the spirit out of it. I'm very fortunate to have enough money to keep me in modest luxury till the end of my days, and have a wonderful niece like you to come and visit me so often.'

Dee smiled; this was more like the aunt she knew. 'I'm not sure there's such a thing as modest luxury,' she said. 'But I must confess we're all easier in our minds knowing you're safe in a centrally heated building, where there are people around and good food to eat. You deserve a little bit of being waited on with no worries.'

When they arrived at the pub, they were given a window table by the smiling waitress who had been welcoming Louisa for years. 'They've kept this old place going quite nicely,' commented Louisa without bothering to lower her voice. 'Some of these places get quite conveyor belt like when they become part of a chain, but this one's surviving so far.'

The waitress exchanged glances with Dee. 'I'll find out if there's a choice of soup for you, my dear,' she said to Aunt Louisa. 'I know you're not keen on tomato.'

'Thank you so much,' said Louisa. Then to Dee: 'You see what I mean — so obliging. Now what will you have to drink?'

Aunt Louisa had a small glass of house red with her lunch. It was her one little indulgence she said. The doctor allowed for it, in the tablets she was obliged to take, in order to keep her blood thin.

'Don't know how Arnold is,' remarked Louisa as their plates were being removed. 'Hasn't been to see me for a while. Probably researching one of those books of his.'

'Arnold? Oh, Arnold,' said Dee, remembering Arnold Turnbull who had bought Brook House from her aunt.

'Of course that Arnold, such an old fashioned name, how many Arnolds do you think I know? He's probably wrapped up in all his military history. Last thing I heard he was writing on the Battle of Waterloo, as if we didn't have enough written on that subject already. It amazes me that he makes enough to live on. I mean, military history, it's hardly lucrative, surely? I hope he's keeping the house in a good state of repair. I didn't sell it to him so he could neglect it.'

'I tell you what,' suggested Dee after they'd enjoyed their lunch and she'd allowed Louisa to pay the bill because she could see argument would be fruitless. 'Why don't we drive past Brook House? We could call in there if you like, see how he is.'

Louisa's face lit up. 'Could we? Could we really?'

Quelling the urge to check her watch, Dee grinned. 'Of course we can,' she said.

But in the end, they didn't call in. Dee pulled up off the road so that they could look up the gravelled driveway to the front of Brook House.

It was indeed a beautiful house, thought Dee. Beautiful, but showing definite signs of neglect. The paintwork on the upstairs sash windows was peeling. The small porch roof had a couple of tiles missing and there was a rusty, green stain on the masonry below, where one of the gutters was obviously blocked or leaking. Oh dear, perhaps not such a good idea to come here after all.

'Lovely, Deirdre, isn't it?' Aunt

Louisa was feasting her eyes on the view before her.

'Yes, it is,' agreed Dee suddenly realising that of course Louisa's eyesight wasn't quite what it used to be. Best not to comment on the fact that the tatty curtains in the upstairs windows were still drawn at two-thirty in the afternoon. Or mention that the drive was full of weeds and the shrubs so overgrown, that she'd be hard pushed to negotiate the car past them in places.

'I don't think we'll go in, Deirdre, if you don't mind, I'm a little more tired than I thought. But, it's just lovely to have seen it again. It looks so mellow. Well, I suppose it would, it was built in Regency times; it's nearly three hundred years old. We had some good times here, my sisters and I. Not all good, of course, but on the whole . . . ' her voice tailed off as she continued to look mistily through the window.

'Jane and Ann's ashes are scattered down by the brook you know, and mine will be too when the time comes.'

Wondering just how Aunt Louisa had that figured out, Dee held her breath.

Louisa gave a sudden dry chuckle. 'It's all right, I haven't suddenly gone ga ga. It's all been arranged with Arnold. I made it a condition of the sale, and he was quite ready to comply. He's a good ten years younger than me, fit as a fiddle and with my heart condition, well, being realistic — he's bound to outlive me . . . Yes, I've shown him the place. It's along the bank where the old rhododendrons are. Lovely spot, I'll be happy resting there, with the brook flowing past.'

'Aunt Louisa, stop it! You're not to talk like that.'

Louisa chuckled again. 'I'm sorry, you're quite right. It's very naughty of me, specially as the doctor said the other day I had the lungs of an eighteen year-old-and a brain like Einstein, mind you, I think he might have been exaggerating a little there.'

Dee grinned. 'I can't believe that,'

she said slipping the car into gear and preparing to pull out. 'I'd say your brain's sharper than Einstein's if anything.'

Louisa chuckled. 'Well, of course, Einstein was a mere man, I have the advantage, being a woman.'

'That's strange,' Dee said staring into her rear view mirror after she'd pulled out.

'What's strange?'

'A BMW has just pulled into the drive of Brook House.'

'Nothing strange about that. I suppose poor old Arnold's entitled to a visitor from time to time. Dull as ditch water though he may be.'

Dee didn't have the heart to tell her that, to her eyes, Brook House had not only looked neglected but totally uninhabited to boot.

Now Jack knew that, beyond all shadow of a doubt, he was becoming obsessive. He must be, because when he'd seen the small silver Mercedes, just exactly like the one his dream girl had been driving that very morning, his heart had started beating at ninety miles an hour and he'd practically driven his brand spanking new BMW straight into the back of it. He'd braked in time, of course he had, he had excellent reflexes. All the same it had given him a jolt.

Fortunately, he'd just managed to catch sight of the person in the passenger seat, who looked to be an old girl on the verge of eighty or thereabouts and in no way a likely buddy for his dream girl.

You've got to stop this Jack, he told himself sternly. Now get on with the matter in hand and have a look round this house that you're lucky enough to have got wind of early.

He left his car at the bottom of the drive and walked slowly up the rise to the front of the house. It was stunning. Jack felt the first stirrings of excitement. It was Regency built, beautifully proportioned, classic and simple. The windows in the three stories looked over the front grounds and, as Jack gazed up at the roof and chimneys, the sun slid from behind a cloud and bathed the pale-stuccoed walls with a warm wash of light. Wow! Jack wanted this house.

First of all he walked all round it, assessing it with an estate agent's eye. He looked for signs of damp, for dry rot, woodworm, cracks, subsidence. Anything in fact that would detract from its value before he got too excited about the interior. It all looked pretty sound. With his anticipation mounting still further, he let himself inside the hall. Oh, glory be!

The staircase was the original wrought iron, rather like the one he'd seen in the Brighton Pavilion, but plainer and black. The ceiling cornice was intact and the door locks original. Scarcely daring to breathe, Jack pushed open door after door. Wonderful ceilings and light fittings; a pair of dilapidated French doors, a bay window that let in streams of golden sunshine; the reception rooms were a dream. He pushed on to the back of the house and the kitchen.

Yes, well. The kitchen was a mess. Dreadful nineteen seventies units lumped in next to a beautiful built-in dresser that had to be original. An ancient chipped butler sink, with wait a minute — a pump, poised over an old wooden draining board! Surely no one in the recent past could have been living like this! Then he spotted a more up to date stainless steel sink next to the pump arrangement. Good, they'd had the sense not to have the old features removed.

A small pantry containing a further butler sink, and a scullery, complete with an old-fashioned bell system display box over the door, also led off the kitchen. Jack could scarcely contain his enthusiasm. With some careful thought something wonderful could be done here.

He ventured up the staircase. It felt pretty solid. He couldn't get over how light flooded the upper rooms. In spite of the brook at the end of the garden, that had given the house it's name, the house itself was situated at the top of an incline in remote splendour and consequently was bathed in a light and airiness that was almost magical.

Now, come on Jack, this isn't like you, he instructed himself again. One of the first lessons he'd learned in the property development business was that it didn't pay to become emotionally involved with a property. And up until now, he never had. He gave himself a shake, before exploring further.

Even the rooms on the topmost floor were of good size, square, light and some with small fitted cupboards, some with gas fires which looked as though they'd been fitted in the nineteen thirties. The wallpapers were pretty hideous, but that was no problem — no problem at all.

Jack was beginning to revise his initial intention of gutting the building and turning it into three quality flats. He knew he had the reputation of being a bit of a Philistine, because he could not subscribe to the theory that any building was beautiful purely on the grounds of being old. In the past he'd transformed some horrendous old Victorian houses that had little more to recommend them than strong building lines outside, which hid a succession of dark, poky rooms on the inside. Dark and poky, just didn't sell. Jack knew that, and if a building had a preservation order on it, he was the first one to scarper, not barter.

But, glancing around Brook House once more, Jack knew that this could be made beautiful. It didn't need to be turned into three luxury flats; it didn't want to be. This house was worthy of the full treatment. It deserved to be turned into a stunning family home once more. It cried out to be restored to its former glory.

But back in his car, a crease appeared between Jack's brows. A project like this would take money, time and dedication. The dedication he had in spades, but time and money, almost the same thing in Jack's book, well they could end up being a bit of a problem. And at the end of it, how many families would be in the market for a seven bedroom house?

Unable to suppress a rueful smile he shook his head. He was getting a bit before himself, again. It was bound to go to auction. This kind of house, a one off, always did, and when it did, he would almost certainly be outbid.

3

Attempting to push her hair from her forehead with the back of her hand, but only succeeding in spreading wisps of pink from her nose to her hair line, Dee stepped back from the bedroom wall in order to survey her handiwork.

It was all coming along very nicely. The flat was generally in good decorative order, but for some reason the landlord had decided on a dreadful dirty grey for the main bedroom walls. Dee preferred something more girly and set about changing it within a week of moving in. It was looking good.

The flat was great and she felt at home already. True, so far she only had a bed, a side table, an old sofa convertible and a coffee table, but she'd soon have a few shelves up to house her music centre and her CDs. Luckily, the kitchen was a fully equipped refit and the bedroom had a built-in wardrobe, so all she needed was a computer desk, and bookcase, a few rugs and she'd be in business.

With the four remaining weeks of the holidays stretching before her, Dee felt she was ahead of her targets and had plenty of time to relax and enjoy herself before knuckling down to the new school and new school year.

Of course, she had been sad to leave the old school, in a way. But she hadn't minded leaving London. When she'd first moved to London, she'd enjoyed the buzz of living in the big city, but somewhere at the back of her mind, she'd always hankered after Devon's soft air. Devon, with its Mediterranean atmosphere, its lush countryside and its vivid rust coloured soil, which had been cultivated at least as far back as Celtic times. Somehow Devon, Dawlish in particular, would always be home.

Dee's contemplation of her whisper pink wall was rudely interrupted by the sound of the phone.

'Hi,' she grabbed the phone at the same time as removing a splurge of paint she'd just noticed on the skirting board.

Then she froze mid motion, staring at the ooze of pink paint staining her paint rag. 'Oh no!' She sat down rather suddenly on the floor. 'Yes. I understand . . . Nothing you could do . . . No pain. No, well, that's the important thing . . . It's just so hard to believe . . . Yes, just two days ago. I brought her here to see my new flat. She — she loved it . . . No, it's OK. I'm all right really. You say my dad knows? He's coming down? Yes, of course. I'll ring him right away . . . '

For a few moments, Dee stayed sitting on the floor staring at the phone. It couldn't be true? Could it? Not Aunt Louisa, who had twinkling eyes, a great sense of humour and the lungs of an eighteen year old. How could she be dead?

Tom and Kitty Stanley arrived late that evening, and although Dee had promised herself she wouldn't, at the sight of her father, she'd burst into stormy tears.

'Oh Dad. D'you think it was my fault? Perhaps I overtired her bringing her here to see the flat. I should have waited until I had it properly finished. I should have thought about the front steps, they were bound to be too much for her.'

'Easy now, easy,' said her dad patting her back. 'First off, she went the way she would have wanted. She always said she didn't want to hang on like an invalid, didn't she? She always said she considered herself to be living on a bonus and she wanted to die with her faculties intact. Well, that's what she did, and of course you're sad. We all are, but it's meant to be, and she'd want you to accept that and get on with your own life.'

'Dad's right,' said her mother in the background.

Miserably Dee nodded, knowing all the time that her own life would never be quite the same, without the knowledge of Aunt Louisa there in the background wishing her well.

True to form, Aunt Louisa had already arranged and paid for her funeral, which went ahead with very little delay. Dee and her father went to Stafford Place to clear up the last of her effects. A few pieces of pretty china were put to one side for Kitty, and Dee kept a tapestry worked footstool and Aunt Louisa's journal. Then she looked sadly round, wondering that there was so little left of the aunt she had loved so much.

'You'd better have these,' said Tom to his daughter.

Dee nodded as she took the small urn, which held Louisa's ashes. 'Yes . . . Maybe next time you come down I can arrange with Arnold for us to scatter her ashes at Brook House. I just don't feel equal to the task at the moment, I'm afraid.'

'Me neither,' said Tom. 'Mum and I have to see Louisa's solicitor, then we have to head back home. Work tomorrow. Life goes on you know. Now, look after yourself. We'll ring when we arrive home.'

Dee squared her shoulders. 'Safe journey, Dad.'

It wasn't until a few days later that Dee looked at Aunt Louisa's journal. It had a Victorian looking cover and illustrations on the borders of every page. Slowly Dee turned the pages and discovered that Louisa had only started to write when she'd left Brook House for 'a life of luxury,' as she termed it, at Stafford Place.

Don't suppose I'll have much to do, she wrote, *so I just have to do crosswords, play Patience and write my journal to keep my brain sharp and myself occupied, only what on earth I'll find to write about, I can't think!*

However, Dee found as she flicked through the pages reading an entry here and there, that actually Louisa had managed to find interest in even the smallest thing, and her life had been very far from empty. On occasion, Dee even found herself laughing aloud at some of her aunt's dry observations.

Then suddenly, there before her, near the end of the used pages, was the entry made on the day they'd visited Brook House.

Oh dear, I didn't say anything to Deirdre of course, but Brook House is looking decidedly seedy. Quite sad really. Couldn't bring myself to go in. Dear sweet child, so keen to please me. I think she was quite shocked too. All those weeds in the drive! Can't Arnold even afford some weedkiller? Lovely old house though, and memories can't be spoiled by a few old weeds. Would dearly like to think I'll end up there — by the brook along with Ann and Jane. Now, I must stop this. Too morbid for words!

Dee fought back tears. 'You will,' she said aloud. 'You will rest there by the brook with your two sisters, with the frogs and the blackbirds hopping around. I swear it.'

The next morning, as she had promised herself, Dee got into her small Mercedes and drove to Brook House. It was raining but muggy, quite usual for August. She felt slightly nervous, aware that this strange Arnold character, even supposing he was still there, might be crotchety and suspicious, and not only would she have to inform him of Aunt Louisa's death but also ask permission to scatter her ashes, and what if he said no!

Resolutely, Dee put this idea out of her mind. Why on earth should he say no? It was a perfectly reasonable request, and one; after all that he'd known all about and agreed to before he'd bought Brook House.

The drizzle had worsened by the time she pulled into the lay-by in front of Brook House. She sat for a moment staring in disbelief through the rain-splattered windscreen, at the obviously positioned auctioneer's board, immediately above the half-opened heavy, wooden gate.

'I don't believe this,' she said aloud. But somewhere deep down, she knew she wasn't really surprised. Last time she'd been here, she had the feeling something was wrong. She should have found out then why the property looked so desolate and neglected. But what could she have done, she argued with herself? Nothing that she couldn't do now.

Dee scrabbled around in her bag for a pen and notebook and wrote down the auctioneer's telephone number. She'd ring them — explain. After all auctioneers were human weren't they? What were a few ashes to them? She'd ring right now, in fact. Right this minute. She scrabbled around a bit more in her cavernous bag and produced her mobile phone.

Less than five minutes later, she had the car in gear, and where normally she would have continued up to the next roundabout before making the turn, did a smart U-turn in the road, and took off at speed for the road to Plymouth.

Three quarters-of-an-hour and forty miles later, Dee looked anxiously at her watch. Today! The auction was taking place today. Any moment now, in fact. Not quite sure what she'd do when she got there, Dee was only determined to be there on the spot when Brook House went to a new owner.

Aware that her heart was beating uncomfortably fast, she parked as near as she dared do to the auctioneer's which, luckily, she knew well from previous visits to Plymouth. Taking her life in her hands she careered across the road, through the high double doors and into the back of a large room which was filled with serious, brochure carrying people, who looked as though they knew exactly what they were doing.

No one bothered to look her way except for the auctioneer himself, who gave her a cursory glance, before peering back through his half glasses at the papers in front of him.

Two houses later and it was the turn of Brook House. According to the auctioneer it was a beautiful period house, a one off. Although in need of renovation, it could be restored into a wonderful family home, or equally into several luxury apartments. It had created a lot of interest and there had been in the region of eighty viewings.

Dee held her breath. The bidding started at a ridiculously low price. For a moment she thought she'd heard incorrectly. If it was going to go as low as that, surely she could, together with her savings, the money Aunt Louisa had left her, a loan from her Dad and a mortgage, she could almost buy it herself. Then reality set in as the price went up in leaps and bounds and one by one the bidders dropped out.

The sale of Brook House now seemed to be resting between Smart Suit with mobile phone and Hideous Sweater with smiley eyes. Both looked to be in their thirties.

Dee hoped that Hideous Sweater would win, but not as much as she wished that she had just won the lottery and was also in the bidding.

'Sold to the gentleman at the back with the telephone!'

Oh dear! Just what she'd hoped wouldn't happen! Smart Suit gave a satisfied smirk and left the sales room. Determinedly Dee followed right behind him. She caught him in the foyer, just as he was about to leave the building.

'Excuse me, my name's Dee.'

Smart Suit turned to her, with a 'do I know you?' expression, which was immediately irritating. Determinedly Dee smiled. 'Um, the house you just bought, Brook House that is, well, it used to belong to my aunt. Before it belonged to Arnold, I mean.'

'Oh yes?' He couldn't have sounded less interested.

'Yes,' went on Dee resolutely. 'Actually she's just died. Just last week actually.' She swallowed, get a grip Dee, you're repeating yourself.

'Right and?'

Dee gulped. This was really hard work. 'Well her dying wish. Well, not actually quite her dying wish, but her expressed wish . . . You see she had this agreement with the last owner Arnold, um — I can't remember his name but Arnold someone or other, he writes military history . . . Well, anyway, she had this agreement that when she died, her ashes would be scattered in the garden. Because she and her sisters they used to play in the garden, and they were so happy together and well, they're already there, you see . . . The ashes of the two sisters . . . '

Smart Suit's phone was ringing. He turned away and answered it. 'Sure,' he said into the receiver. Then turned back and made a careful viewing of her, from top to toe, just as though she were some old house up for renovation. Biting her lip, she stood her ground.

'Sure, will do. Yep, sure thing. Oh, tell me about it! Traffic! Nightmare or what? Yep, sure . . . Got to dash.' He slid his mobile back into his pocket. 'You were saying?' he said, looking at her with a more appreciative expression but one that made Dee long to tug down the hem of her skirt and pull up the neckline of her T-shirt.

'My aunt,' she struggled on manfully. 'Is it possible that I could scatter her ashes in the garden of Brook House? I'd just have my mum and dad with me. We could do it at your convenience . . . '

Smart Suit's phone was ringing again. 'Sorry, can you hold a moment,' he said into the receiver. Then, not bothering to disguise his impatience he turned back to Dee. 'D'you know who I represent? No, I can see you don't. Lumsden's Developments. Ever heard of them? No? Well, the policy is. Buy 'em up. Knock 'em down or gut them. Refit and sell them on at a profit. It's called business. We don't have time to waste.'

'Well, couldn't you just ask?'

Smart Suit laughed as though she was a not very bright five year old. 'Fraid not,' he said. 'I know the answer already. They'll be moving in contractors and machinery any time soon.

Can't have Joe Public wandering round scattering ashes. We're not insured for that kind of thing. Sorry!'

He turned away to attend to his phone again, and blinking rapidly to stop her tears from dislodging her contact lenses, Dee pushed past him through the doors and into the street.

Jack had parked his BMW at a funny angle. The reason for this was because some idiot who just so happened to own a small silver Mercedes had also parked at a funny angle thereby affecting all other cars in the immediate area. Jack refused to speculate that the owner of the Mercedes could possibly be his dream girl — he was in business mode.

He'd got the house; he'd actually got it! Wow! Not even having to park the BMW in a slip-shod way could upset him. He pressed the key tab, heard the car lock behind him and glanced over his shoulder, because that was what he always did. But before he'd had a chance to look back again he felt a thump on his arm as a small dark-haired figure, with a huge bag on her shoulder, pushed past him.

'Hey, where's the fire?' he said.

'Sorry,' she mumbled when she'd recovered her balance. 'Bit upset, wasn't looking where I was . . . '

'Oh!' interrupted Jack hardly daring to believe his eyes. Oh happy eyes! Oh happy day! First the house, now the girl of his dreams!

Only the girl of his dreams didn't look exactly joyous. Decidedly unjoyous, in fact. But first things first.

'It is you, isn't it?'

The girl struggled to compose herself. 'Depends who you mean by you.'

'The you I met, in May . . . At a wedding? I don't know whose wedding, because I wasn't invited. I was at another wedding and I just saw you through the doorway and well, you know the rest . . . I've been looking for you ever since.'

'You have?' She stared at him very hard, as though she wasn't quite sure he was telling the truth.

Jack stared back. The same dark hair, the same even features and sweet expression. Only today something was clouding her dark eyes. She was near to tears, well, actually she'd said something about being upset as she'd brushed by him. She hadn't meant to be rude, obviously not. How could the girl of his dreams ever even think of being rude or inconsiderate?

Besides she was such a light little thing she'd barely touched him really. He smiled, a concerned smile. He had been in a hurry to get to the auction rooms and finish up the business, but this changed things.

'You look as though you could do with a cup of coffee a bit of a chill out. Would you?'

'Yes,' she said, looking slightly shell shocked.

Jack chose soft chairs in the coffee shop. His companion took a couple of sips of her cappuccino then glanced across at him with a shy smile. She tucked a piece of stray hair behind her ear.

'I'm sorry I didn't recognise you straight away . . . I must look a mess. And I'm sorry I barged into you like that. I'd just had a bit of a disappointment, that's all.'

A disappointment? What kind of a disappointment, Jack wondered. To do with a boyfriend perhaps? Almost without realising it, he hoped the boyfriend was now an ex-boyfriend. 'Oh?' he asked politely.

'Well, I'm more angry than anything. Furious in fact. I mean, some people are so heartless, so unfeeling.'

Sympathetically, Jack nodded, convinced that anyone who upset the wonderful girl sitting opposite him must be heartless and unfeeling and deserved a flogging at the very least.

'I mean, my aunt — right? Never hurt anyone. Lived in that house all her life, until she was forced to sell through ill health . . . All she ever wanted was to rest in peace alongside her sisters in what she considered to be her home. What possible harm could a few scattered ashes do to anyone?'

Jack was feeling a little puzzled. Perhaps he'd missed something while he'd been dreaming over his dream girl's dreamlike profile. On the other hand he very definitely hadn't heard the word boyfriend, ex or otherwise.

'Er, no,' he said. 'Certainly not.'

'Oh goodness, of course. You've absolutely no idea what I'm talking about.'

'Well, yes. I mean, no.' Actually he hadn't, any more than he had a clue what he meant. All rational thought seemed to go out of the window as soon as she fixed him with those deep, dark, soulful eyes.

'My name's Dee,' she said holding out a small tanned hand.

Feeling slightly short of breath, Jack took her slim fingers in his. 'Hello Dee. My name's Jack. Jack Lumsden.'

Dee began to smile, then something went terribly wrong. The smile died and a fire kindled in her eyes. 'Jack? Jack Lumsden . . . did you say Lumsden?'

'Er — yes.'

'As in Lumsden Property Developers — Lumsden?'

'That's right.' But it wasn't right, it was obviously very, very, wrong. He didn't know quite what or why, but this conversation had definitely taken a turn for the worse.

Shakily Dee stood up. 'Monsters like you shouldn't be allowed to do business,' she said in a trembling voice. 'You're heartless — pitiless. And I know I should feel sorry for you and your kind — always chasing the next buck. But I don't. I hope your business fails and you get what's coming to you . . . What goes around, comes around . . . Don't forget that. Goodbye Mr Jack Lumsden.' Dee gathered up her monstrously large bag and made for the door. 'And if I never set eyes on you again, it would be too soon,' she said over her shoulder.

Stupidly, Jack stared at the two cappuccinos sitting cosily side by side. Where had he gone wrong? Why was she so angry? He became aware of some teenagers sniggering over in the

59

corner and felt an angry flush staining his cheeks.

All he'd done was treat her to a coffee. What right had she to be so angry? A half smile tugged at his mouth. It wasn't as though he hadn't suggested decaff. It wasn't as though he'd force-fed her. Honestly, women! She'd cannoned into him with that outsized bag of hers, really hard as a matter of fact, his shoulder felt quite sore, he might even have a bruise. And had he complained? No. She'd accepted his ready sympathy, the offer of friendship and a coffee, then stormed off with absolutely no explanation.

No, Jack. You were right the first time. Women and you don't mix. You might like them, but they don't like you. And as for understanding them . . . Well!

4

Now calm down and be reasonable, darling.' Dee drummed her fingers on the kitchen surface and changed her phone to the other ear. 'Mum, I am calm . . . Look, no offence, but let me talk to Dad.'

Kitty Stanley gave the sigh which, from long experience of telephone conversations with her mother, Dee had come to expect. 'He's not in, and even if he were in, he'd say the same thing.'

'Fine, I'll ring him on his mobile.'

'It's switched off. He's on the golf course.'

'Oh.'

'Honestly darling. This ashes thing, it's no big deal.'

'It is to me.'

Another sigh. 'Well, there's no hurry is there?'

Without answering, Dee drummed

her fingers some more.

'I'm sure this property person will be ready to co-operate when he's had a chance to think about it . . . You took him unawares, probably rushed in like a bull in a china shop.'

'Thank you, Mother.'

'Well, you know what I mean. You're not always the soul of tact. Wait a couple of days — give Dad his telephone number, and he'll speak to him, man to man, and explain.'

What? Man to man? Where on earth did her mother get her outdated ideas and expressions from?

'Believe me. Jack Lumsden is not that reasonable.'

There was a pause. Dee waited for the sigh.

'OK, darling. Well, my program's starting in a minute . . . Just try and relax a bit, that's all.' Ah, now the sigh. 'And try not to get so passionate about things.'

'I'm not passionate,' said Dee in a voice verging on the hysterical.

'Well, wound up then. You do tend to overreact . . .'

'OK, Mum, I'll call later when I've had a cold shower or three. Bye now. Enjoy your TV.'

Dee clicked off her phone and wearily sat down on the second hand kitchen chair it had seemed such fun to paint lime green to match her tea-towels.

Was she overreacting? Had she gone about it all wrong? Should she have waited, approached the new owner at a more appropriate time?

Maybe her mother was right for once and a more subtle tactic was called for.

She got up from the tiny kitchen table, painted white, because she'd had to concede it was possible to overdo the lime green, and started to pace about the flat, her face flushing as she tried to recall the exact words she'd used in her conversation with Jack Lumsden. Well, actually she couldn't really call it a conversation. She seemed to recall she'd hardly given him a chance to speak.

The idea of Brook House being

demolished was so upsetting, and the thought of poor Aunt Louisa hardly in her grave, or her urn, as it were, and Mr greedy Lumsden already set to destroy her childhood home, had just overwhelmed her. Thinking about it even now was enough to make her shake with rage.

He'd been so smooth, so pleasant and she had to admit it she had been very, very excited and yes, even happy to meet again, the dark stranger with whom she'd shared that one dreamy dance. It had been romantic and thrilling. But it was all a sham. He'd just pretended to be nice, pretended to be sympathetic and all the time he was at the very heart of her misery — the root cause.

Yes, she'd had every right to be angry. Every right.

A block of soulless flats rising up from a concrete car park, where the old shrubbery had been established; she shuddered, it really was beyond belief.

But, flats or no flats, Jack Lumsden

or not, somehow or other she had to fulfil Aunt Louisa's wish and scatter her ashes.

Jack's BMW travelled sleekly along the road to — the house. Brook House. His house. He couldn't prevent a small, satisfied smile from playing at the corners of his mouth. He'd wanted it and he'd got it. The finances had gone through and he had the keys in his pocket.

True, Si had been the one to do the actual bidding, but Jack was the one on the end of the phone giving instructions. In the end he'd deemed it wisest not to attend the auction himself, he was too well known in the sale rooms and some of the other bidders might have gone the extra few thousand in order to outbid him. It wasn't often Jack Lumsden paid over the odds for a property, but Brook House was different and if he'd been there he just might have been tempted.

It was a shame about his dream girl, who'd turned out to be not so much a dream girl, as a barking mad girl. When Jack had eventually caught up with Si he had been told about some hysterical female accosting him after the sale.

'Said she was old Arnold Turnbull's niece.'

'Didn't know he had one,' said Jack. 'Only the nephew — Roger Turnbull and he's the one put the house up for auction. That's how I understood it anyway.'

'Well, she was a nutter,' said Si, 'going on and on about sprinkling his ashes in the garden.'

'Oh,' said Jack making the connection. 'Her surname might be Turnbull then?' Dee Turnbull. He wondered what the Dee could be short for.

'Dunno,' answered Si whose phone was ringing again. 'Obviously a sandwich short of a picnic. Shame though, she was a bit of a looker.'

Thinking of this now, Jack felt a small flutter under his ribs. Ignore it, he told himself firmly. This was no time for him to have a female in his life, especially not an unpredictable one. Brook House had come at no small price. He'd had to let out his own, originally Georgian but tastefully converted, fully furnished, flat, situated in a posh part of Teignmouth, in order to meet his financial requirements. So, to all intents and purposes, until he could get a shower functioning in Brook House, he was homeless.

Or would be if it weren't for his sister, Kim. She'd put him up for a few days until he got himself sorted.

But now, here in all its glory, was the house. The heavy wooden gates had been jammed open. Deftly Jack turned the BMW through them. The overgrown shrubs were encroaching over the worn, used to be gravelled, drive to such an extent that less than ten yards in, Jack had to stop the car for fear of scratching the bodywork.

He got out and looked back at the gates. He'd have to secure those for a start. The last thing he wanted was squatters. Humming softly to himself, he took the house keys from his pocket and walked on up towards the house.

★ ★ ★

'Well, I've found Prince Charming, only he's not a prince and he's singularly lacking in the charm department.'

Gina straightened herself from her reclining position on her sun lounger and stared at her friend in disbelief. Quite aware of her scrutiny, Dee continued to lie passively back on her cushions without giving away her thoughts by so much as the twitch of an eyebrow.

'You've found him? Why didn't you tell me?'

Dee gave a small shrug of her shoulders. 'Nothing to tell. Non-event . . . Anyway I'm telling you now, aren't I? And we didn't take to each other. Not at all.'

Gina looked at her through half closed eyes. 'Oh no?'

'No, he's a money grabbing, awful, awful person.'

'Oh well, if that's the case . . . '

'It is the case.'

'How did you come to that conclusion? Spent much time together have you?'

'Enough,' said Dee enigmatically.

The two sun loungers were placed together side by side on a small patch of concrete immediately outside Gina and John's kitchen. Temporary or not, it caught the sun's rays for most of the day and as Gina's husband, John, had gone to a cricket match, the two girls were engaged in chatting, relaxing and topping up their tans.

'Tell me,' said Gina. 'You know you're dying to.'

So Dee told her about Aunt Louisa, about Brook House, about the auction and Smart Suit winning the bidding.

Gina was sympathetic. 'But where does Prince Charming come in?' she asked after an appropriate pause. 'And how did you recognise him?'

'I'm short sighted not blind, Gina. I didn't recognise him, he recognised me.

Then of course, when I looked properly I could see it was him. Anyway, there was his voice . . . ' Dee's words trailed off as she remembered him saying, 'It is you, isn't it?' in exactly the same tones as 'Dance with me,' and the accompanying quiver that had shivered down her spine.

'So, what was he doing at my wedding? Uninvited, I might add.'

'He was at another wedding and he saw me from the doorway, as he was going past.'

'Well, I suppose I should feel a bit miffed,' said Gina sounding completely tranquil. 'After all he gatecrashed my wedding! The nerve of some people. But I still don't see why you should hate him.'

'Because he's bought Brook House and he . . . he's going to tear it down and make it into prison barracks and he won't let me scatter Aunt Louisa's ashes in the garden.' Dee's voice ended on a wobble.

'I'll make a cup of tea,' suggested

Gina, 'or would you rather a gin and tonic?'

'I'm all right, really. I'm a bit upset that's all. I was just getting myself nicely sorted out. You know, put Ray and the past behind me. New job about to begin, new flat; I had plans to take my aunt out more, make new friends, and it just doesn't seem as though I've got off to a very good start.'

'Hmm, new friends indeed! What's wrong with the old ones then?'

Dee gave a watery smile. 'I'm counting on you, believe it! I've got to figure out a way to scatter the ashes yet.'

Gina disappeared into the kitchen only to reappear a few minutes later carrying a tray containing two cups of tea and a plate of chocolate digestive biscuits.

'I knew there was a reason you were my friend,' said Dee tucking in.

'I've been thinking,' said Gina after rearranging herself on her sun lounger.

'Why not, just do it?'

Dee didn't pretend not to understand. 'I thought of that. It just seems wrong, that's all. And my mother would have a fit. She'd probably have me locked up. She thinks I'm hysterical and out of control. She sent me a book on coping with a failed love affair along with a little note advising me to eat plenty, I ask you? Do I look as though I'm fading away?'

Watching as Dee reached for her third biscuit, Gina had to shake her head.

'And honestly, I'm so over Ray . . . I haven't thought of him for weeks. I don't think I was ever really in love with Ray. I was in love with the idea of being in love, if you know what I mean.'

'And he was fun.'

'And he was fun.'

'And of course, the accent helped.'

'The accent actually got on my nerves a bit in the end . . . No, I think my pride was hurt more than my heart. It was only infatuation.'

'What does your dad say?'

'Oh, he's very laid back. Never liked Ray anyway.'

'No, I meant — about the ashes.'

Dee pulled a face. 'Well, by the time Mum had got to him he decided it was best to go along with her. Told me not to make things difficult for myself. That Aunt Louisa is dead now so it makes no difference to her anyway.'

'He has a point of course.'

'I know, but . . . '

'But because you're stubborn and because you're you, you're going to find a way, aren't you?'

'Oh yes,' said Dee reaching for her fourth chocolate digestive. 'You bet! And as for Jack Lumsden. I'm not giving him another thought.'

'Mmm, I can see that,' said Gina.

5

Black jeans, black long sleeved T-shirt, trainers and a baseball cap into which she'd scraped her hair; yes, she looked about right.

Of course, her hands and face would stand out like white blobs, but on the whole Dee had decided that boot polish as camouflage paint was a no no.

'Spoil sport,' Gina had said petulantly. 'First of all you won't let me come and now you refuse me the fun bit of making you up. Honestly, it's like you don't trust me or something!'

'Gina, much as I appreciate the offer; firstly, two people stand twice as much chance of being caught as one. Secondly, this is my thing, and I sort of want to do it quietly and on my own. Thirdly, you'd turn it into a comedy act and if anyone were to be around they'd hear us giggling even if they didn't see us.'

Gina looked hurt and put her hand to her chest. 'Moi?' she said in injured tones. 'A comedy act . . . I wouldn't. I'd treat it with great seriousness and respect.'

Dee sighed. 'I'm sorry, Gina, but you know that isn't true. And there is a funny side I know, even I can see that, but well, I'm better doing this on my own.'

'At least let me be your driver then. I can sit in the car outside and keep cavey for you. If I see anything I can hoot like an owl as a warning cry, like this . . . ' She proceeded to put her hands to her lips, mouth organ fashion, and with crossed eyes, gave a wavering *too-wit, too-woo*.

Dee grinned. 'Well, that should frighten every cat in the neighbourhood, it certainly frightened me.'

'What about dogs?'

'No, I don't think it would frighten dogs. Well, maybe a very small one.'

'No, what I mean is, and I'm being serious this time, dogs as in guard dogs. Ah, hadn't thought of that, had you?'

Thinking of this now, a slight frown appeared between Dee's brows. Guard dogs! Although she'd pooh poohed the suggestion at the time, she had to admit they were a real possibility. Eventually, she'd promised Gina that if there was a guard dog warning posted, which she believed that, by law, there had to be, she would abandon the idea of venturing into the grounds of Brook House at all.

But even if she was planning to trespass on private property, she told herself firmly, she had very good cause, didn't she? Surely, there was no judge in the land who would actually send her to prison when she was just carrying out her aunt's dearest wish?

So, now she was ready. It was late evening and overcast. Lighting up time was fast approaching. She'd decided not to leave it too late, partly because although she was going to take a torch, she didn't really want to use it, but mostly because she had to own up to the fact that wandering around alone, at the dead of night was a scary prospect.

For the last time, she ran through her checklist. Mobile phone turned off naturally. Torch, car keys and most importantly, the urn containing the ashes, sitting in a canvas bag attached to a short length of rope. Right, OK, well — everything going according to plan then. Come on Dee, get on with it.

Once in the car, she felt calmer. As she approached the house she was unsure what to expect. Ever since the auction, she'd avoided going past it in case she saw anything terrible happening, which would upset her still further and maybe weaken her resolve.

She pulled up in the lay-by in front of the house. The heavy wooden gates were still wedged open, but in front of them some metal security gates had been put in place. For a moment Dee was nonplussed, she hadn't bargained on scrambling over eight foot high security gates. Never-the-less she got out of the car and peered up the drive. In the gloom, she could just about distinguish the back of a BMW.

She focused on and upwards towards the house and could dimly make out, what might or might not be, scaffolding against the front elevation. Well, she thought with relief, at least Brook House hadn't been bulldozed flat. Not yet, anyway.

The house looked dark and empty. But she hadn't expected any frantic activity at this time of night. She was quite surprised after seeing the security gates, that from the front, at least, there was no sign of a security light. Then she wondered briefly about the BMW, decided that even if it did belong to Jack Lumsden, it might be parked there as being a 'safe' place while he used one of his countless other cars.

For a moment Dee wondered whether she should do the sensible thing and go home, put it off till another night, when the BMW might not be there. But tomorrow she started her new job, tomorrow, she would be Miss Stanley to a class of seven-year-olds, and Miss Stanley didn't break the law by trespassing. No, it had to be tonight. It had to be now.

Aware that her heart was hammering quite hard, despite the fact that she hadn't actually even done anything yet, she licked her dry lips and contemplated Plan B.

Plan B involved driving on another fifty yards or so and parking her car at the entrance to a field opposite the boundary wall of Brook House. Having done this, Dee switched off the engine and the car lights then sat and thought about the next step, which certainly equated to breaking and entering.

Well, not the 'breaking' part perhaps, she thought a few minutes later, having grabbed an overhanging branch of a walnut tree and rubber-soled it up the brick wall like a monkey. Her next move she contemplated seated somewhat precariously on the top of the brick wall where, sheltered by the tree's branches, she had often whiled away the time in the long summer days of her childhood.

Barely stopping to think of this now she dragged the canvas bag, complete with its precious contents, up behind her, then slowly lowered it down the inside of the wall. Well done for thinking of a Plan B, she congratulated herself. She landed with a soft thud on to the piled up leaf mould at the foot of the tree, next to the ashes, and inside the grounds of Brook House. Now the 'entering' part was behind her. She listened intently. Good, no dogs, as yet.

But her breathing sounded unnaturally loud, so she forced herself to stand quite still until she became used to the idea of being here in the old garden once more, then tried to work out her exact bearings.

Oh dear, now she could just make out a chink of light in the building. She estimated it was coming from the kitchen area around the side. Dee frowned. It was probably only a light on a timer, to keep trespassers like her away. It wouldn't make sense to employ a night watchman or guard dogs unless there was building equipment worth stealing, and Dee certainly couldn't see anything fitting that description at the moment.

Uneasily, she recalled the BMW, but having come so far, decided it was too late to turn back now.

Stealthily, and hugging the wall as much as possible, she edged farther round the side of the plot towards the back of the garden, which was where she knew the brook ran. Progress seemed to be extremely slow. It was quite dry underfoot and apart from the occasional car going past on the other side of the wall, there was a silence that made every cracked twig sound like a gunshot.

The chink of light must have been a reflection, Dee reassured herself, because it seemed to have disappeared now. The bulk of the house was dark and silent. As silent as the grave, so when there was the sudden sound of a door opening, the whine of a rusty hinge, followed by a cough, Dee's heart jumped straight into her throat area.

Quickly turning her face to the wall, she froze in her tracks. Right now, the face paint idea didn't seem like a bad one. Why was she doing this? Did she have a death wish? Still scarcely daring to breathe she heard a dustbin lid rattle, then the door hinge again and the rasp of badly fitting wood against wood, as the back door closed.

So, unless doors opened by themselves, and managed to cough as well, someone was there. Dee could hazard a guess as to who that someone was. Should she turn back, abandon the project? Yes, it was the only sensible option. Of course she should.

And she would, in a minute.

Eventually, she risked a glance towards the house where, in spite of a dim light, as though a door further within had been left open, all looked to be quiet. Slowly she released her breath. Oh for goodness sake, she could do this. She wasn't a wimp. Now she knew the dangers, she'd just have to be more cautious that was all.

The next bit though, was going to be a little bit tricky. Somehow, she had to round the corner, then negotiate the walled kitchen garden, which backed on to, naturally enough, the kitchen and more importantly, the kitchen window. Which, if someone happened to be glancing out of it, would put her smack in the frame, so to speak.

The top half of the kitchen door was made of obscured glass so that was OK, no one could see through that without X-ray vision. Inch by inch Dee moved slowly through the kitchen garden just beyond the pool of light that escaped the curtainless window. Hopefully it was dark enough outside and bright enough inside for her to be barely noticeable, but this had to be the worst bit, just had to be.

As she stepped outside of the kitchen's beam Dee heaved a small sigh of relief. From now on it should be plain sailing.

Crash!

Oh no! She'd tripped straight over a heavy galvanised watering can. Clutching the urn to her chest she scrambled up, hotfooted it straight on through what was left of the kitchen garden, over the overgrown lawn and into the cover of the shrubbery, heading straight for the brook.

Behind her she heard the door with the rusty hinge open with another screech and then a security light flooded the area up to the shrubbery. Wondering if you could actually die from fear Dee crouched down low amongst the azaleas.

Maybe, whoever it was in the house, would think it was a cat that had made the noise. A very heavy footed, clumsy cat. She suppressed a smile. If Gina were with her she'd be mee-owing like mad by now. A moment later and she heard the door shut again. She didn't dare look in case the light picked up the paleness of her face.

She remained on her haunches with her knee cramped under her for a couple of minutes, then very cautiously moved forward, still stooping, until she reached the gentle slope that would end at the brook.

Another ten yards and she reached her destination. The rhododendrons had long since finished flowering and there was a dank smell of peat and rotting debris, but the ambience was one of peace and tranquillity. Dee could hear the brook now. It was slow flowing at the moment, just a gentle murmur, but she could remember playing here at times when the waters had been swollen to the extent where the banks had been flooded.

It was quite dark now, but there was no sound of pursuit so she risked turning on her torch in order to retrieve Aunt Louisa's ashes from the cumbersome urn. Slowly, she shook the feathery flakes of ash over the ground beneath the rubbery green foliage of the largest rhododendron.

'You're home now, Aunt Louisa. Rest in peace,' she whispered.

After standing quietly with her head bowed for a few moments, Dee addressed herself to the next problem. How to get out.

Jack stared into the darkness beyond the range of the security light. He'd pulled the door to behind him and was standing, one step beyond the kitchen, in the gentle night air. The fox or cat that had disturbed his enjoyment of half a beer and cheese sandwich, would be long gone, he knew that. If it was a fox, or cat.

For Jack had glimpsed a movement on the borders of the shrub area, rather higher than your average fox could stretch to. About five foot higher. He kept very still, his senses tingling with the feeling of time suspended and someone else out there in the grounds, his grounds, who had no business to be there.

Go easy, Jack. People carry knives these days. Getting killed for the sake of a few scrumped apples would not be sensible. But Jack wanted to know, just who was in his garden. He didn't have a torch. But he didn't figure on needing one. He knew the grounds fairly well by now. Knew that the shrubbery went back to the boundary wall and there was no easy way out there.

The only other option was down by the brook. You'd have to get your feet wet to go that way, and then brave the mass of brambles and stinging nettles that skirted the field on the other side. But his trespasser might not know that.

As silently as possible Jack made his way to the boundary wall and started to work his way along it till he met up with the steeper slope that led to the brook. Nothing. Then, just as he was about to give up and go back to his cheese sandwich, he heard a slight scuffle. Of course it could have been a fox but somehow it sounded human. Anyway foxes didn't swear under their breath and carry torches.

Or wear baseball caps, for that matter, he thought an instant later, as the part silhouette of a young skinny lad came into his field of vision.

'Got you!' Jack's hand shot out and grasped the lad by the shoulder.

A strong hand grasped Dee's shoulder. Oh no! She lost her footing, landed on her stomach, with her nose pressed into a mound of leaf mould. At least she hoped it was only leaf mould!

'Get off me!' she yelled trying to free her hands which were caught in a vice-like grip behind her back.

'All in good time,' came Jack's voice. 'First I want to know what exactly you're doing on my property.'

Dee struggled until she could move her head enough to see a pair of battered trainers topped by a rather excellent pair of bare legs. The beam of her torch, which lay discarded next to her nose, enhanced the legs. Wow! Even Gina would be impressed by those legs. Her eyes travelled a fraction higher. She was quite relieved to see that just above the knee the legs disappeared into frayed cut-off jeans, in the same state of disrepair as the trainers. Some men should never wear shorts, she thought, but Jack Lumsden was not one of their number.

The legs took a step back. 'OK, you can get up now.'

A little unsteadily, Dee rose to her feet and Jack picked up the abandoned torch and shone its light straight into her face momentarily blinding her.

'Well, well,' he said. 'It's the crazy lady who never wanted to set eyes on me again. What made you change your mind? Bit extreme isn't it, accosting me on my own property, or could you just not wait a moment longer?'

'I didn't change my mind,' Dee said sulkily putting a hand up to protect her face. 'Since you chose to be so unco-operative I had no option but to try to carry out my aunt's wishes in secret.'

There was a long silence. 'I won't pretend to know what you're talking about,' said Jack thoughtfully, 'but you're starting to shiver, you'd best come in and have a hot drink.'

Dee shook her head. 'No thanks,' she said. 'I've done what I came to do. I'm sorry I've taken your time up. I'll be going now.'

'I don't think so! I think I deserve an explanation . . . Anyway how did you get in? Don't tell me you vaulted over an eight-foot fence!'

Dee grinned. 'No, I stayed here a lot when I was a kid. I know ways in you'd never think of in a million years.'

'You used to live here?'

'No, I told you. My aunt did. Well, my father's aunt, so that would make her my great aunt. It was a family house. My aunt lived here with her two sisters . . . Oh I've told you all this.'

'No you haven't. All you told me was what kind of coffee you wanted.'

'Oh!' For a moment Dee was nonplussed. Hadn't she told him? She thought she'd explained. 'Well, if I didn't tell you it must have been your henchman I told. He didn't want to help me either.'

'Hold on a minute. Help you with

what?' Jack sounded genuinely puzzled. 'No don't answer that, at least not until we've got out of here. What's the quickest way back to the kitchen?'

'That way.' Dee pointed. 'There's a faint path between the shrubs. I really don't want a hot drink. I'll go out the way I got in.'

As she spoke Dee slipped out of the beam of the torch which had become quite feeble by now and started at a smart pace for the safety of the walnut tree and the boundary wall. She could hear Jack behind her, but she had the advantage of knowing exactly where she was going and he didn't catch her until she had one leg on the bottom branch of the tree.

Once more she felt his vice-like grip on her arm. 'No you don't,' he said.

'Oh, yes I do,' answered Dee kicking out with her other foot. A moment later she realised that lifting both feet off the ground at once was not a wise thing to do. Doubly unwise when the strong arms of Jack Lumsden were only too ready to catch her as she fell. Her baseball cap fell off and her hair tumbled out. Her body was pressed very close to his and her nose was level with his chin.

His mouth gave a twisted smile. 'We must stop meeting like this,' he said. 'On the other hand . . . '

His mouth came nearer. It was a very nice mouth. Dee felt slightly dizzy. His lips brushed hers, and somehow she couldn't draw away. Then she didn't want to, because the kiss was firm and sweet, gentle and exhilarating all at the same time, and something deep down inside her was telling her that this was exactly how she'd known his kiss would be from the very first time she'd seen him.

Then, like a cold wet flannel in the face, reality took over. What was she doing kissing a strange man in the depths of a shrubbery late at night? The wrong thing, obviously.

She'd regained her footing now and Jack had relaxed his grasp. With a hard shove, she pushed Jack away, turned with the quicksilver movement of a cat and shinned up the tree and over the wall. A smothered curse came from behind her, but she didn't pause in her sprint for the car.

She was panting by the time she reached it. Practically crying with relief, she felt in her jeans pocket for her car keys.

But they weren't there. Too late she remembered she'd put them, along with her phone and the urn, for safe keeping in the canvas bag. The canvas bag, which right now was still at the foot of the walnut tree, on the wrong side of the brick wall.

6

Jack could not believe it. The dream girl-come-crazy lady had done it again. She'd scarpered. And he still didn't know her full name; still didn't know why she'd suddenly abandoned him in the café; still didn't really know what she had to do with this house, his house.

It took him a couple of seconds to think all this and recover from the kiss, which after all, had been some kiss. Then he set about going after her up the tree. At least that was the plan. Only, as he grasped the nearest branch and prepared to spring into action in a fair imitation of the Tarzans portrayed in old films on TV, but perhaps without the yodel, he stubbed his toe against something hard and unyielding.

After a curse or two, because he guessed he'd never catch her now, he bent to pick up the toe stubber, which proved to be a heavy object wrapped in a canvas bag. He loosened the rope at the top of the bag, peered into its depths and, with the aid of the torch, managed to discern a strange looking vase. Unbidden, the sharp memory of his grandfather's funeral came to the front of his brain as he recognised the vase for what it was — an empty urn.

He frowned, all sorts of warning bells going off in his head. Dimly, he remembered Si telling him about the bizarre conversation he'd had with Dee, concerning ashes and the scattering thereof. Surely that hadn't been what she was doing, had it?

Oh Lord. Why on earth hadn't she just asked him? But then again creeping about in secret was just the sort of crazy thing she would do, he thought, still staring into the bag. There was a glint of metal at the bottom. Gingerly, Jack put his fingers in and felt around. He found a mobile phone and, oh joy, he'd found her car keys!

With a renewed surge of vigour Jack swung himself into the tree dragging the bag after him. By the time he dropped to the other side of the wall, she'd long gone. Jack wasn't perturbed, he was reasonably sure that she'd have parked her car just off the road at the entrance to a field, it was the only possible parking place on this particular stretch of road other than outside the security gates he'd put up.

Holding the torch in front of him in order to warn drivers of his presence, Jack started up the road at a leisurely pace.

Sure enough, fifty yards further on he found her slumped against the side of her car looking very sorry for herself.

'You may be needing this,' he said passing her the bag containing the urn and the phone. 'And these,' he added holding up the car keys.

'Thank you,' she said shouldering the bag, extending her hand for the keys and looking as though she couldn't quite believe her luck.

Jack held the keys above his head. 'Not so fast . . . I think I'm due some kind of explanation.'

Dee gave him her startled fawn look and Jack's insides turned to water. Why did she have to look at him like that? It was unnerving and made him forget what he was going to say next.

'My friend, my boyfriend, will be here soon,' she said. 'Any moment now, actually.'

'Will he?'

'Yes, he will . . . He's six foot two and he's an ex-boxer.'

'Really? Not much of a boyfriend I'd have thought, if he lets you do this sort of thing by yourself.'

Dee licked her lips. The lips he'd so recently kissed. Struggling to keep cool, Jack watched fascinated. 'Well, it wasn't his fault, he well, naturally he wanted to come, but well, he suffers from a phobia . . . Arbouri-phobia . . . '

'Arbouri-phobia?'

'Yes, fear of trees.'

Jack gave a snort of laughter. 'Fear of

trees? Funny I could have sworn that was tree-aphobia. But maybe it's wall-aphobia, or crazy woman-aphobia he suffers from. I might suffer from that too after tonight. OK. I'll give you your keys. But you have to promise not to keep running out on me. I swear to you, I'm not dangerous . . . '

'You felt a bit dangerous to me, pouncing on me like that, and . . . '

'And what?'

'And . . . kissing me. What on earth did you think you were doing?'

'I don't know. It wasn't premeditated I assure you . . . Anyway, you were doing it right back . . . Enjoying it in fact.'

'I wasn't.'

'Oh, I think you were.'

Dee made a sudden lunge for the car keys and by some stroke of luck managed to wrest them from him.

'You should have asked me about scattering the ashes, if that was what you wanted to do. I'm a reasonable sort of bloke . . . '

But Dee was in the car now, the engine was on and Jack found himself stepping backwards in order to avoid ending up in the casualty department of the nearest hospital.

Almost hysterical with relief, Dee parked the Mercedes, and let herself into her flat. She'd done it. She'd actually done it.

She looked at her watch and sent Gina a text. *Mission accomplished — no sweat.* Then she wondered what to do next. Not that she didn't have plenty to do. She had to organise herself ready for the first day of term tomorrow, she had to have a shower and hair wash. Goodness yes, she had loads to do.

Strange then that she didn't feel more at peace, more content. Strange that actually she felt quite restless, as though she was sorry the evening had finished quite so quickly. Strange that she should keep thinking about that overbearing, ruthless, advantage-taking Jack Lumsden.

And that kiss.

Jack didn't have the keys to the security gates with him, so in the end, wall-aphobic or not, he had no choice but to go over the wall and back through the shrubbery in order to get to his curling cheese sandwich and slightly flat beer.

He looked round the kitchen. Apart from a microwave cooker, a two burner hob, a small pine table and chairs and an old sagging sofa, it looked very little different to when he'd first bought the place. So far he'd rigged up a basic shower in the corner of the butler's pantry, which he planned to change into a downstairs cloakroom, he'd had the electrics made safe and hooked up the plumbing to a new boiler. In the dining room he'd temporarily installed his bed and a sturdy clothes rail. Brook House was now habitable, but only just.

Just as well, thought Jack, registering anew the dilapidation of the place, just as well really that Dee had turned him down on his offer of a hot drink. It was obvious she didn't think much of him already and if she were to witness the way he was living at the moment she'd think even less.

And just why should you care what she thinks of you or your living arrangements, he asked himself. Si was quite right. Dee was nothing short of a nut case. But even so Jack knew that he did care, he cared very much indeed.

The first week of the school year, always felt longer than any other week. Dee knew that. But even so, it had been an enjoyable week. The school was small and friendly.

Some of the staff were more reserved than others but that was always the way, and the children, well, Dee had always loved children and it didn't take long for them to respond to her natural warmth.

By Friday, she knew all their names, which ones needed firm handling, which of the girls were the fussy, chatty ones, which boys had an excess of energy, and those children who might be in need of some extra TLC.

By Friday she was also so exhausted that all she wanted to do was call in at a supermarket, pick up a take away and have an early night.

Late Friday afternoon was not an ideal time to go to a supermarket, Dee found, some fifteen minutes later. But her trolley was pretty full so she resigned herself to wait at the check out, hoping that none of her pupils would be on a weekly shop with their parents.

After a race with the till operator who, once having established that no help was required with packing, seemed determined to beat the world record in till totalling. Dee emerged into the hazy six o'clock sunlight and made her way to her car.

Oh no! Despite all of her resolves, that Jack Lumsden was not a person she wanted to impress; the mere sight of him at the boot of his BMW, parked next to hers, was enough for her to smooth a hand over her hair and to wish she'd worn the pink, instead of the grey T-shirt today.

'Hi,' said Jack as though she were an old friend of some standing.

'Hi,' replied Dee because it seemed rude not to.

'Funny I should bump into you.'

'Yes, I'm hysterical.'

'Here, let me help.' Jack handed her bags to her after she'd opened her car.

'Are you following me, or what?' Why did I say that, she thought a second later? There's no call to be so rude to him.

Jack just grinned. 'No, well, not exactly. I was on my way to my sister's place and I just happened to see you pull in. Honestly. And I thought well, it's daylight, perhaps you'd explain.'

OK, smile. Try to be nice, or at least polite. If her heart would just behave and not start beating overtime, the way it always did whenever Jack was in the vicinity. 'Nothing more to explain,' she said without looking at him. 'Brook House used to belong to my aunt. She

103

had an agreement with the last owner, Arnold Turnbull, that her ashes would be scattered there by the brook along with those of her sisters.

'She never thought that she would outlive him, she was so much older, you see! As it happened, she didn't outlive him by much, but it was enough.' She did look at him now, straight in the eye. 'Enough for the developers to move in and tear the place down and forbid the scattering of ashes due to health and safety regs.'

Jack narrowed his eyes. 'Hold up,' he said. 'If by 'Developers' you mean me, you couldn't be more wrong. I'm not tearing the place down, I'm trying to restore it to its former glory, and I didn't forbid the scattering of ashes. If you'd given me half a chance I'd have been only too happy for you to hold a complete remembrance service if that was your wish. Only, where I come from, it's polite to make the request first.'

Stony faced, Dee continued to pack

her shopping into her boot.

'Look let me show you the plans,' went on Jack, opening his car door and dragging out a folder. 'These are the plans of Brook House when I bought it, and the proposed changes, which, other than basic modernisation to make the place habitable, are very few.'

The plans were a temptation Dee couldn't resist. Before long she was peering over his shoulder as he pointed out new drainage systems, alterations to the downstairs layout at the back of the house, areas of repointing to be done and possible changes in the kitchen area.

'The great thing about Brook House,' said Jack stabbing his finger where the large hallway showed on the plan, 'is that although it's old, it's got light. The light just floods in from that wonderful window at the top of the stairs and goes everywhere. You must have noticed it. It's Regency, you see. Can't beat Regency for style. Then the Victorians came along with their long dingy passageways, and small claustrophobic rooms. Some of those just cry out to be gutted. I wouldn't house my prize canaries in them, let alone modern families . . . '

'Funny, I wouldn't have put you down as the canary breeding type.'

Jack grinned. 'See, I knew we'd get on. Same sense of humour.'

Watching his animated expression as he elaborated on his plans, Dee felt a wave of relief wash through her. 'I thought you were at the very least going to convert it into flats,' she said.

'No, not this one' said Jack. 'It's going to cost me a fortune and take me years, but it's such a wonderful house with so much character it deserves to be brought back up to scratch. Tell you what, you should come round and see it some time. You must be able to remember what it was like when your aunt lived there. Your input would be invaluable.'

Dee wrinkled her nose. 'I don't know. I think I'd be better leaving my memories intact. Anyway, I'm really busy right now.'

'Ah, with the six foot two, tree-hating boyfriend I suppose?'

'Something like that.'

Jack looked disappointed and for a moment Dee weakened. But then he shuffled the plans back into his folder. 'Well anyway, think about it. Take my card. Phone whenever, and we'll fix a time.'

He pushed his business card into her hand and Dee turned and got into her car.

It was only as she was driving away that she realised that the ball was well and truly in her court now. She knew an awful lot more about him than he did about her, and that included her ability to contact him, where he had no idea of her address or phone number. She wasn't sure she liked it being that way round.

Jack had hardly parked outside the small terraced house of his sister, when a seven-year-old boy hurled himself at his legs. 'Uncle Jack, you're late. I thought you'd be here ages ago. My teacher says it's very rude to be late.'

'Does she now,' said Jack who was becoming heartily sick of hearing about Josh's teacher's thoughts on every subject under the sun.

Kim was at the front door and rolled her eyes heavenward. Jack kissed her on the cheek then stood back as Kim dextrously turned her wheelchair in the space of the hallway. He often wished as he watched Kim complete the awkward manoeuvre, that he'd had just a little more space to play with when he'd converted this particular house.

'How's things,' he asked a couple of minutes later when Kim had lit the gas under the potatoes and checked on the juicy and succulent smelling chicken that was in the oven.

'OK thanks. No pain today, if that's what you mean. I've done most housework below waist level and a bit of feather dusting. Josh and I have made the beds between us and Colin should be home soon. Oh, I've got a physio session Tuesday of next week, Colin will be away working from Monday, and Mum's busy, so could you be an angel and pick Josh up from school?'

'Sure,' said Jack. 'No problem. Will you be OK, Monday morning?'

'Yeah, Josh and me, we'll be fine, and after school Monday, my friend Cathy's, picking him up, so everything's hunky dory.'

'Good,' said Jack, because even though he knew that being paralysed from the waist down was anything but hunky dory, there wasn't very much else he could say.

'Uncle Jack shall we play football?'

'I was just hoping you'd say that,' said Jack with an ironic grin at his sister. 'But is it a good idea to play football just before dinner? What would your teacher say about that?'

'Miss Stanley would say exercise is very good for you, but it's good to give your tongue a rest sometimes,' replied Josh.

'Hmm,' said Jack, who on the whole didn't care for teachers much. Not any of the ones he'd met so far anyway. Smug beings in his experience, who generally thought they knew everything and couldn't wait to tell you so. 'Well, I suppose that sometimes she could be right . . . Now, you going to be in goal or d'you want to be attack?'

'Attack, attack!' shouted Josh gleefully.

7

'So, you're not planning on seeing him again?' Gina asked, staring intently into Dee's eyes.

'Not planning to, no.'

'But he's got good legs!'

'Ah yes, there's that to consider.'

'And you liked him, didn't you?'

'I didn't say that.'

'You didn't have to. You get this gooey look every time you mention his name.'

'I don't!' said Dee indignantly.

'Oh yes, you do. I think it's lovely. It's so romantic.' Gina batted her eyelashes and adopted a high-pitched, little girl voice. 'Oh, Mr Rochester — you're so tall, so handsome and you've been so understanding about my scattering my aunt's ashes in *her*, I mean *your* garden.'

Dee batted Gina on the head with a magazine. 'If you're going to take the micky, I won't tell you any more.'

'Ah, so there is some more.'

'Well, only that I met him in the supermarket car park.'

'And?'

Dee flushed. 'And I was rude to him. Accused him of following me. I mean why? Why would I do that?'

Gina chuckled and took a sip of her cappuccino. 'Because you fancy him rotten, that's why. It's all your defence mechanisms kicking in. You're fighting the biological attraction. But that's good, it will be so much more rewarding, so much more passionate when you finally give in.'

Dee snorted, then stared at Gina for a long moment. 'Thing is Gina. I don't know if I will see him again. I've got his business card, but he knows nothing about me. Only my first name . . . Coincidences apart, and we've had more than our fair share of those already, there's no way he can find me.'

Gina struck a questioning pose. 'Oh dear, that could be a problem. Never mind. I'm sure love will find a way.

You, for instance could always call him . . . You know, on the phone for example — Dumbo!'

Dee didn't answer.

It was Tuesday. Jack checked his watch. Although he'd left the office in plenty of time to pick Josh up from school, the term was still quite new and he wanted to be absolutely sure that he would be right there waiting for Josh in the playground. He knew what it was like to stand waiting and waiting.

He knew what it was like to have a variety of different people who were not your mum, because your mum was working, to saunter along ten minutes late and pick you up from an impatient teacher and an otherwise empty playground.

When eventually he reached the school, he was surprised to find some other blokes clustered at the school railings. He'd thought he'd be the only one, but should have realised that what with mums working and men doing shift work, lots of dads would be fetching their offspring from school.

For a moment he wondered what it would be like to be a dad. He thought he could probably bear it if his son were like Josh for instance. Then, before he could start fantasising about who the mother might be in this interesting but slightly scary scenario, a door in the school building opened and children, dragging school bags behind them, came hurtling on to the playground.

There were so many of them. A lesser man might have panicked, but Jack skimmed his eyes backwards and forwards about three and a half foot from the ground searching for his nephew's tousled head. Trouble was, lots of boys had tousled hair of a nondescript brown shade. Jack felt the beginnings of a worried frown form between his eyebrows.

'Uncle Jack!'

Oh, the relief. There he was, running towards him. Shoes half undone, jacket all askew — Jack would have known him anywhere.

'Hang on, Josh,' called a feminine voice and an arm stretched out and yanked at Josh's collar.

Jack looked at the slim, lightly tanned arm. Somehow it seemed familiar. His eyes travelled on up to a slender neck with dark brown hair just curling in towards the side of a pretty profile. Jack knew that profile. He'd thought of nothing else night and day for months.

That and the fact that, because he was an idiot and hadn't had the presence of mind to take her phone number, he still didn't know how he would ever get to see that profile again.

'You've dropped your school bag,' said Dee.

Josh made a grab for it.

'Hold it . . . ' said Jack. 'What do you say?'

'Thanks,' muttered Josh. 'This is my uncle.'

With a ready smile on her face Dee turned towards Jack. To Jack's speechless delight, her eyes widened, so did the smile and he was almost sure a blush was creeping up her neck.

'Hello, Uncle,' she said. 'So you're the famous 'my uncle can do everything'.'

'Seems so,' said Jack who was still struggling with the idea that Dee could actually be Josh's teacher.

'OK. Well, I had a call from Josh's mum to say his uncle was picking him up, so I had to hold on to him till last so he could establish you really are his uncle. We have to be careful you see.'

'Of course,' said Jack. 'I quite understand. And you're Miss?'

'Stanley,' put in Josh. 'I told you before. I told you a million, trillion times.'

'So you did,' said Jack, who had never before been interested in anything remotely connected with teachers, let alone remembering their names.

'I can't see Mummy!' A little girl was dragging at Dee's other arm.

'I expect she'll be along any moment now,' said Dee turning her attention away.

'Wait!' Jack hoped she didn't notice the pathetic note of desperation in his voice.

Dee looked at him over her shoulder. It was a questioning look, tinged maybe with a vestige of hope, or was he fooling himself?

'Please give me a call. Or better still, let me ask you to dinner or something.' Now why had he said that? She'd never come to dinner with him, never in a month of Sundays. And what about the boyfriend?

'That is, if there isn't really a six-foot-two boyfriend?' he added.

She was definitely blushing now as her startled fawn eyes met his. And dared he to hope that there was an expression of relief in them? 'No, the boyfriend was spur of the moment fiction . . . But you must have guessed that . . . ' She paused. He held his breath. 'OK then. I'll give you a call tonight.'

'Great,' said Jack fighting the idiotic grin taking hold of his features. He placed a firm hand on Josh's shoulder and guided him out of the playground.

'Uncle Jack,' said Josh in his clear, high-pitched child's voice, 'why are you smiling and why has your face gone so pink?'

'Shush,' said Jack.

Dee examined her reflection in the mirror and scowled. The trousers were fine. They fitted in all the places they ought to, making her legs appear longer than they actually were and were a rather subtle shade of sludge. It was the top half that was the trouble.

The white round necked, cap sleeved effort made her look exactly what she was, a sensible schoolteacher with no social life to speak of. Pathetic! What about the turquoise? No, she dismissed it at a glance, she fancied the neckline had rather too much of the vamp about it for a first date.

The pink, which was her favourite, was out of the question now she'd suddenly noticed how faded it looked. Oh well, it would have to be the bold geometric print in black and white, which had just enough sludge incorporated in its design to stop her looking like a draught board.

Anyway, why was she making such a fuss? It was just a bit of supper. That's what he'd said on the phone in his sexy, deep velvet voice. 'How would you feel about coming to Brook House and I'll fix you a bit of supper, and I can explain my plans for the place . . . But, if not, well, we can go somewhere else. I'm easy. Well, no, you know what I mean. I'm not fussy. No, that's not what I meant either . . . I'm not good at this, am I?'

And what had Dee said? 'You're doing fine,' then she'd given a nervous laugh. 'I'd love to come to supper and I'd love to see Brook House again.'

Taking the cap from her lip-gloss Dee applied two careful coats of succulent pink to her full lips. Should she have played harder to get? Should she have suggested that they meet in a pub? Had she made it too obvious that, as Gina put it — she fancied him rotten?

And how was she going to cope in the oversized house that used to belong to her aunt, with only Jack and a few possible mice for company? He'd explained that he only had a minimum of furniture, to make it comfortable to work there.

He just wanted to see her in order to pick her brains about how Brook House used to look, that was all. He wasn't interested in her, as in interested in her date wise, of course not, after all he'd only just asked her name, had never bothered to take her number. Brook House was what they had in common, probably all they had in common.

It would be interesting of course to listen to his plans and if it turned out to be a fun evening too, that would be a bonus. She didn't have to care what she looked like — not at all. Definitely not!

And after all, it had been easy.

She'd known it would be of course!

★　★　★

When she arrived, she found the heavy wooden gates opened wide in a welcoming gesture. She parked her car behind his and walked towards the front door but, before she could reach it, Jack came towards her from round the corner of the house bearing two glasses and an already opened bottle of wine. He was wearing jeans and a white polo shirt, open at the neck. His hair was wet as though he'd not long had a shower and as Dee leaned forward to take the glasses, she caught a whiff of nutmeg and some other intangible something which made her want to stand nearer and sniff deeply.

Control yourself, Dee, wouldn't Gina just smirk to see you drooling?

'It's such a lovely evening, I thought we'd have a drink on the patio,' said Jack leading the way round to the west facing dining room terrace.

This part of the garden hadn't changed much. Jack had given the gently sloping lawn a rough cut and the overgrown shrubs poured over the edges in the way they always had. Two rusty wrought iron chairs and a matching table had been set with a plate of olives, a dish of oil and balsamic vinegar and some crusty bread.

'Have a seat,' said Jack indicating the least rusty of the two chairs. 'Sorry I haven't got any cushions. The tea towels are clean though, my sister does my washing for the moment.'

Rather gingerly, Dee sat down on the spindly chair with its tea towel cushion. The French doors to the dining room were open and the strains of music coming from a beat-up portable radio seemed somehow appropriate.

'This is lovely, very civilised,' said Dee, tearing off a hunk of bread and dipping it into the oil.

Jack looked up from pouring the wine. His eyes met and held hers for what seemed a very long moment.

'You know I think this picture must have been in my mind the very first time I saw this house.' He gestured behind him. 'The sun dipping down over those trees, their last rays hitting the French doors, a pretty girl sitting here, just as you are, sharing a bottle of plonk with me.'

It was a magical moment; so perfect that Dee was frightened anything she said would spoil it. She was back in Cinderella land again with a tall, dark stranger asking her to dance.

But she wasn't quite ready to be a Cinderella. This was real life. Wake up.

She gave a half laugh. 'Well, you started well, almost poetic. Shame you called it plonk — not wine.'

Jack grinned. 'Would you like to see where you scattered the ashes?' he asked. 'In daylight, I mean?'

'Yes I would.'

So, with a glass of Merlot in one hand and a hunk of bread in the other, Dee followed Jack across the lawn and along the bark path that led between the shrubs down towards the brook.

'Peaceful spot isn't it?'

'Yes,' agreed Dee. 'That's why she chose it.'

'I wouldn't mind ending up here myself, what with the brook bubbling by and the odd frog or bird hopping around.'

Dee froze with her glass halfway to her lips. 'What did you say?'

'Well, I wasn't being serious — I mean, hopefully I have a few years to go yet before I start to think about things like that.'

'No, I didn't mean that bit. It's just what you said about the frogs and the birds hopping around. That's almost exactly how Aunt Louisa put it.'

'Well, well, perhaps we have more in common than you thought. Perhaps your aunt wouldn't mind my having bought the old place after all.'

'No,' replied Dee smiling. 'D'you know, I don't think she'd have minded one bit!'

Supper was good. The pasta was only just about cooked enough, the sauce came out of a bottle and the green salad came out of a bag, but none of that mattered.

The evening had developed a chill so they ate in the kitchen, one each side of an old pine table, lit by a line of tea lights on the windowsill. Without the harsh fluorescent tube, that was the only other lighting in the kitchen, the dereliction of the room wasn't quite so apparent.

Jack gave her a guided tour of the rest of the house explaining as he went what he planned to do with each room, how he intended to leave as many original features as possible.

'You're actually living here then?' said Dee, eyeing the bed in the dining room a trifle wearily.

'Yep, buying it stretched my resources somewhat. Temporary cash flow problem.'

'Oh.'

'Property developing is all about balancing your budgets. I've rented out my apartment in order to finance this project, which is going to take a long time by the looks of things.'

'What will you do with it when it's finished.'

Jack looked away from her. 'Unfortunately, unless my circumstances change, I'll probably have to sell it . . . Now let's have some coffee. Only instant, I'm afraid.'

Dee made the coffee, while Jack cleared the table. Then they sat on the old sofa that was squeezed into a kitchen recess, looking at each other over the rims of their coffee mugs.

'What's Dee short for? Delilah? Delicious? Delightful?'

Dee gave a groan. 'Deirdre,' she said, 'and I hate it.'

Jack burst out laughing.

'You're not meant to laugh. Most people just say 'oh yes,' and change the subject. You're not very sensitive are you?'

Jack shook his head in mock disbelief. 'Deirdre,' he repeated. 'Well, I must admit I prefer Dee. But Delicious, or Delightful would be equally apt, and I warn you, that's the best I can do in the sensitivity department.

'You know I feel as though I've known you for years,' he went on. 'I can't believe I've only just met you.'

Dee curled her feet up under her and settled more comfortably on the sagging sofa. 'Neither can I . . . Although strictly speaking we met back in May.'

'And I'm so surprised you're actually single.'

Tossing up whether or not to tell him about the Ray episode and deciding that on the whole 'not' would be best, Dee gave a small smile. 'Well, you know how it is — men never make passes at girls who wear glasses . . . What about you?'

Jack examined his fingernails before tossing off a laugh. 'Well, you know what they say — he travels fastest, who travels alone. Anyway, I haven't seen you wear glasses, I suppose you wear them for reading?'

'No, I wear contacts and I wear them all the time. Well, nearly all the time. I didn't have them in when I met you. Hence I thought you were a wedding guest I hadn't noticed. I drove everyone mad afterwards trying to find out who you were!'

There was a long silence.

I've blown it, thought Dee.

'Ah, so you were trying to find me,' said Jack with a note of triumph in his voice.

Dee could feel her face flaming. 'No, not really. I was only curious as to who you were and that you weren't a figment of my imagination. Of course it never occurred to me you were nothing but a common gatecrasher!'

Jack put down his coffee mug, and his face was suddenly very close to hers. She could see a small scar on his upper lip; feel the heat of his body through his shirt.

'Gatecrasher, maybe,' he said. 'Common, never. And do I regret it? No, not one little bit.'

Funny really, thought Dee slightly haphazardly. Gina was so right about the red-hot passion just taking over when you stopped fighting your feelings. Then she stopped thinking and gave into the sweetness of the moment as Jack's lips descended on hers.

8

'TYPICAL!' Dee washed her hands in the sink before answering her phone with her still damp hands. Honestly, it wasn't often she got involved with the cooking thing, and now just when she was enjoying it, she was rudely interrupted.

'Hi,' she said somewhat shortly.

'Darling, just ringing to see if you're OK,' came her mother's reproachful voice.

'Yep, I'm fine.'

A sigh transmitted itself down the phone. 'Oh, you're busy . . . '

Dee cradled the phone between her neck and ear and prepared for the long haul. 'No, Mum. Well, not too busy, just getting a meal together for tonight.'

'What are you having?'

Why did her mother always display this insatiable interest in Dee's nutritional diet? 'Only chicken. I'm marinading it in herbs and wine and stuff.'

'Oh, someone's coming then? Gina, I suppose.'

'No,' said Dee feeling slightly stung that her mother seemed to think she possessed only one friend in the world. 'No, actually, it's Jack.'

'Jack!' her mother repeated.

'Don't say 'Jack!' like that. He's very nice.'

'So you keep saying. Seems a bit of a sudden, radical change to me, that's all. One moment you hate him, next thing he's the best thing since sliced bread. You're so extreme darling.'

Dee gritted her teeth. 'First of all we've been seeing each other for about six weeks so it's hardly sudden. Secondly I seem to remember you telling me Jack was probably a very pleasant, reasonable person if I only gave him a chance, and now I am doing just that, you don't like it . . . ' She gave a laugh that sounded a little forced. 'There's no pleasing you is there?'

Another sigh.

Dee grinned. *Gotcha, Mum*, she thought. 'Anyway, we're just friends, it's not serious . . . And enough about me — how's Dad?'

Twenty minutes later she put down the phone and caught herself giving a sigh of relief, which sounded remarkably like her mother's. Hastily she changed it into a stretch of her shoulders. She was after all feeling a little tense.

It was the middle of October and the first time Dee had asked Jack round to her flat. At first this had been a deliberate strategy on her part, as though by inviting him into her home she would be admitting to herself just how serious her feelings for him were becoming.

She considered she knew a lot about Jack Lumsden now. For instance, she knew that even though he was a successful property developer, he was also a very good brother to his disabled sister, Kim, and a hands on uncle to Josh.

She knew, from the things Josh had told her about Uncle Jack re-fitting their house after Kim's accident and how he'd spent many hours with him while Kim and Colin slowly came to terms with their new lifestyle. She knew that Jack, apart from being a workaholic, was a man who considered his family above all things and always had time for those he loved.

Yes, the things Dee had found out about Jack over the last few weeks had been surprising and to his credit. Somehow she hadn't expected a hard headed business man, which was after all what he must be to have done so well and so quickly, to be quite so — well, decent.

That was it — decent. An old fashioned term but one that unquestionably described him. Decent, but not in a goody, goody way; more in a wildly attractive sort of way.

Dee sighed again, because maybe, just maybe, it was possible to be too decent. When she'd reported to her mother that Jack and she were just good friends, it was nothing less than the truth. Over the past few weeks, she'd seen Jack a couple of times a week. They'd been to the cinema twice, or was it three times?

Also, he'd taken her to one of his sites; made her wear a hard-hat, explained the intricacies of pile driving, and the beauty of a wiring diagram. Fascinated, she'd studied his rugged profile as he'd discussed the project progress with various workmen on site, and she'd noticed the easy camaraderie that flowed between them mainly due to Jack's ability to lighten any atmosphere with a smile and a joke. And slowly she discovered that she'd like more from their relationship; slowly she'd allowed herself to fall a little in love with him.

They'd been for a long walk on the dune-backed sands of Dawlish Warren; holding hands, talking, laughing and listening to the screech of the gulls. All very romantic but culminating only in a brief hug and kiss and 'sorry, got to dash', before Jack sped off leaving her standing outside her flat door like a jilted bride. Well, perhaps that was overstating the case, but definitely the feeling was one of being let down.

That was two weekends ago. In the week following, they'd gone for dinner in Aunt Louisa's favourite pub. Dee had arrived quite early but Jack had been ten minutes late with paint on his wrist. 'Sorry,' he said. 'I'm still trying to crash on with Brook House but time, it seems, is against me.'

'What's the rush?' asked Dee examining the menu and wondering if it would be very greedy to go for starter, main and dessert.

'There speaks the girl who's never had to live through a winter with no carpets or central heating.'

'Well, I've stayed at Brook House at Christmas as a matter of fact, and they used to have oil fired central heating then. It wasn't brilliant, but it took the chill off.'

Jack shook his head. 'Gone, all gone,' he said. 'Anyway, no oil to run it with. The old oil tank leaked away the remains of the oil at least five years ago and the radiators are all corroded. No, it's been bearable through summer and autumn, but once the winter kicks in, it won't be like 'Five Go Camping'.'

'Oh, did you read Enid Blyton too?'

Jack gave her a hard stare. 'No, I most certainly did not, but Kim did. Anyway, the gas boiler's in, I've insulated the loft, and now we've painted the walls it's time for new rads and pipes. Then I'm afraid the whole thing grinds to a halt.'

'Why's that?'

'Cash flow,' said Jack cheerfully. 'Never mind. I'll be quite snug in the kitchen and dining room once I get the heating going.'

Dinner had been good. Dee couldn't remember exactly what she'd eaten because they'd talked so much about Brook House, about Jack's grandad and his mum, about Dee's family, that the evening had sped by. Then there'd been a lull in the conversation and, just like that, Dee had said it.

'Jack, you know if things do get tough and you're stuck, you can always stay at my place . . . '

And then she'd stopped because a look of sheer panic had spread itself across Jack's features.

'What I mean is,' she'd hastily amended. 'My flat has two bedrooms . . . I only meant in case of dire emergency,' she went on, feeling her face burning like a furnace.

'It's very good of you,' said Jack stiffly, 'but I don't think it will come to that.'

Somehow their conversation had got back to normal by the end of the evening but whereas Dee had been going to ask him back to the flat for coffee, she decided not to after all, and they'd gone their separate ways from the car park.

Then there'd been a series of phone calls. Jack had been busy, much too busy to see her even though he'd been phoning or texting her several times a day.

Now Dee sighed again, and covered the marinading chicken with cling film. He'd suggested they meet at the same pub again tonight to eat, but she'd said no because she was fed up with him insisting on paying when she knew he was broke.

She took a deep breath and invited him to her place instead. And, after initially refusing because he was in no way broke, just waiting for some money to change accounts, Jack had eventually agreed, and here she was wondering just what the evening would bring.

She'd already decided that her best bet was to play it cool. Not frighten him. she mustn't frighten him on any account. If he wanted to be just friends, then that was fine. Why not? She could do friends, some of her best friends were, well, friends.

So, no dressing up. Just jeans, a nice sweater — with a high neck. A polo

137

neck, even. Lighting kept nice and bright; music, jaunty and fun. No songs for lovers, he wouldn't like that. Keep it light, keep it casual. Keep it friendly. Fine, everything would be fine.

9

Jack was so tired he could hardly walk straight. He pulled up outside Dee's flat and groped around under the passenger seat for the bottle of wine he'd brought with him.

Somehow, he'd managed to find time to shower, pull a clean shirt and some jeans from his clothes rail, and clean his expensive boots, which had been purchased in times when he was more affluent.

They were excellent boots made of soft Italian leather. They were a reminder of more carefree days, days before he'd even heard of Brook House or knew of Dee Stanley's existence.

Wearily, Jack smoothed a hand over his forehead in a vain attempt to discard a niggling headache that wormed itself into his consciousness about fifteen minutes ago. It wasn't that he didn't want to see Dee. Far from it, she was there at the back of his mind, night and day, day and night, just like the song said. Only, he wasn't quite sure he was ready for an intense relationship. Not yet. Not right now. But then when he made an effort not to see her, not to think of her, what happened?

He'd just relax a little, be sitting with a cup of coffee, mulling over a drainage problem or some such thing; and suddenly, there she'd be: dancing in front of his thoughts, just like he'd seen her the very first time: in her red dress, with her dark hair swinging and her dark eyes shining.

Then, before he knew it he'd be calling her number or texting her with some stupid joke or thought that had occurred to him and he wanted to share. Jack didn't quite understand what was happening to him, but whatever it was — it was happening way, way too fast.

And now he had a headache, that

could very well turn into a migraine, an aching back, a cut on his index finger that made it difficult to pick up the bottle of wine, let alone open it . . . He was a broken wreck of a man — that was what he was.

The front door opened, and there she was framed in the doorway, with a warm smile of welcome on her face. Her feet were bare, her jeans turned up at the bottoms so she didn't trip over them and she was wearing a soft, blue sweater.

Like a new man, all aches and pains forgotten, Jack fairly leapt out of his car, hardly able to wait to see if the sweater was as cuddly as it looked.

★ ★ ★

'Hi Dee!'

'Hi Gina.'

'You don't sound very high to me. A bit on the low side I'd have said.'

'Oh, I'm OK.'

'Sure?'

'No, not sure really.' This time even

Dee could hear the tears in her voice just waiting to spill.

'It can't be that bad. Tell Auntie Gina.'

'It's Jack.'

'He's never gone and dumped you?'

'No, in a way I wish he had. Anyway, we don't have enough of a relationship for dumping. That's the trouble really. It's as though he's put up a stone wall. Well, not all the time, sometimes I really think we've got something worthwhile you know, but then, he becomes well, very elusive. Oh, I don't know, perhaps I'm imagining it. Just when I feel as though we're on the same wavelength, he retreats again and I suddenly don't understand him at all.'

'Come on, Dee. Buck up. This is called getting to know you time. Getting to know all about you time. I could sing you the song if you like.'

Dee attempted a laugh. 'Please don't! No, you're right. After all we don't really know each other that well. We only see each other about twice a week. He always seems to be working, or seeing his mother or his sister.'

'Have you gone off him?'

'No . . . But sometimes I wonder if he's gone off me. You know, most of the time he treats me like a mate. Then if things start to get in the least bit romantic he backs off so fast . . . It's weird!'

'Probably because you're a teacher. He's showing you respect because he's frightened if he steps out of line you'll keep him in detention or, more likely, start talking wedding dresses.'

'Oh please!'

'Actually, I think it's lovely. An old fashioned courtship! Aunt Louisa would have approved.'

'Aunt Louisa was an old maid . . . A happy old maid — but still . . . '

'Do you still like being with him?'

'Oh yes,' said Dee a certain dreaminess creeping into her voice. 'We have a lot of fun, we really do.'

'I bet.'

'No, we laugh a lot, talk a lot . . . It's just that where at first everything seemed so romantic. Now it feels like he'll do anything to avoid a romantic situation . . . It's very confusing.'

'John's a bit like that. It happens after marriage anyway. Men, on the whole, only use romance as a means to an end.' Delicately, Gina paused. 'No end in sight then?'

'Nope! Came for dinner on Saturday.'

'You cooked for him?'

'I did. He's cooked for me too, once in the very early days, and that time it ended quite passionately, but we were at his place and I felt it was a bit too fast, so it was me who brought that evening to a close. But this time it was at my place and things went really well. Not too obviously romantic or anything like that.

'Then after we'd finished dinner, I was stacking dishes on the draining board and quite suddenly, he came up behind me and started kissing my neck and holding me and telling me how lovely I was, you know all that stuff. We'd had a lovely evening and I could feel myself responding and I really was quite happy about it.

'Then we went back in the sitting room and sat on the sofa and he kissed me again and I thought he was enjoying it, I know I was. Then he gave a sort of groan and said, 'Sorry, I've got to go,' and he went!'

'No!'

'Yes! . . . Now you see why I'm upset! No explanation, no nothing!'

'Have you heard from him since?'

'I've had three texts, all thanking me for a lovely evening and praising my cooking and hoping to see me soon, and he'll be in touch . . . I reckon the ball's in his court, don't you?'

There was a long silence which, it seemed for once, Gina had trouble breaking.

'Reckon so,' she said eventually.

★　★　★

'OK. Let's have some quiet now.'

Harvest Festival had come and gone and now Dee's classroom looked rather as though a hurricane had hit it. There were leaves everywhere. The subject was autumn, and although Dee had had the foresight to suggest that each child bring only four leaves of varying colours, she hadn't calculated for a wet day for collecting them. Now she was faced with upwards of one hundred muddy, soggy leaves to dry out before embarking on the autumn leaf border that she had had such high hopes for.

Oh well, they'd have to concentrate on other things autumnal instead.

'What else happens in autumn?' she asked brightly.

'It gets dark earlier.'

'Good, that's one thing.' Dee wrote it on the board. 'Anything else?'

'The squirrels collect nuts.'

'Yes, the squirrels know the colder weather is coming and store away food for later.' Dee wrote on the board again. 'Now that gives you a clue for another one.'

'I know, I know, it gets colder and it rains more.'

'Yes, we know that's true, don't we?' Dee looked across at the rain-spattered windows. 'Anything else?'

'Start buying fireworks?'

'Well, yes, but it's a little bit early for that . . . Something else happens before that . . . Any ideas for what else happens in two weeks' time, at the end of October?' Dee looked round at the attentive children all struggling to think what she might be getting at. 'OK, I'll give you another clue. Hands up this time. No shouting.' Selecting an orange chalk, she drew a pumpkin on the board.

Suddenly the hands of half the class shot up.

'Josh.'

'Hallowe'en,' he said triumphantly. 'I know about Hallowe'en. It's when the witches come out.'

'Right,' said Dee, who knew from experience that once Josh started talking, it was difficult to get him to stop.

'Yes,' carried on Josh warming to his

theme. 'My Uncle Jack says you have to be very careful at around this time in case one of them gets you.'

The class started to laugh. Dee smiled indulgently. Josh was very popular and the other children were always ready to listen to his colourful narratives. With a cheeky grin he looked round, responding to his audience. 'My Uncle Jack says it's easy to be got, especially if you're a man because sometimes these witches, they disguise themselves as fairy princesses and make you marry them and then they turn back into witches and take all your money and . . . '

'Yes, I think that'll do Josh,' said Dee. 'I think Uncle Jack was joking.'

'No, he wasn't.' Sadly Josh shook his head. 'Uncle Jack married a witch and she did look like a fairy princess, I was page boy.'

In the silence that followed Dee watched a single drop of rain run down the window pane to join the pool on the sill outside.

'Um, yes, right. OK then. Now, I wonder who can tell me three things that we associate with witches. I'll draw one of them on the board for you, to start you off.' Dee drew the body and head of a cat on the board. It was only when she got to the whiskers and the tail that she realised how much her hands were shaking.

10

Somehow, Dee got through the day. Somehow, she kept up a bright conversation with the headmistress, one of her colleagues and the school janitor about heating and windows and the children's washroom floor being left too wet. Somehow, she reached her car and drove to her flat, all without shedding a single tear.

She shut the flat door behind her and leaned against it. Now she was home, she found she didn't want to cry or be sick, she just wanted to punch something, and if it was Jack Lumsden's smiling face — so much the better.

Slowly she sat down on the sofa and examined again the unlikely possibility of Josh either telling fibs or having got it all wrong. But deep inside she knew that Josh had been telling the truth. Boys like Josh wouldn't readily admit to having been a pageboy.

So, why, oh why hadn't Jack been honest with her? The one thing after the Ray episode she'd been extremely careful to have crystal clear, was a potential boyfriend's single status. She didn't do triangles.

Briefly, Dee revisited the grief and the pain she'd endured when she'd found out about Ray's wife. She'd been upset, and very, very angry at being made to feel a fool. But this — this was different. The pain went deeper, because she'd allowed herself to think that Jack was nearly perfect. That Jack wouldn't lie to her. Oh no, not Jack. Jack, after all, was 'decent.'

At least that was the picture he portrayed. Reliable Jack, whose own father had walked out on them all when he was six. Dependable Jack who'd left school early and helped in his grand-father's carpentry business. Hard working Jack, who'd improved his mother's house, bought the house next door when it had been repossessed and improved on that one too, then sold it on at a profit.

Entrepreneur Jack, who'd built a property developing company and never looked back. Busy Jack, who had no time at all for personal relationships. Romantic Jack, who'd asked her to dance the last dance with him, then disappeared. Perhaps she should have taken a warning from that, because what had happened to honest Jack?

What had he said when she'd asked him if he was married? 'He travels fastest — who travels alone.' Yes, well, no wonder his marriage had failed, Dee could just imagine it. His poor wife sitting alone waiting, waiting for him to come home for dinner. Dee could almost feel sorry for her if only she didn't hate her so much.

★ ★ ★

It was Saturday morning, it was early and Jack was starting to worry. Well, not worry exactly; just feel very slightly concerned. He'd tried texting, tried phoning but her phone was turned off, and it had been four days now. Futilely he racked his brains for anything he might have done or said that she could have misconstrued in some way.

Or maybe she'd said something about going up to visit her parents and he'd been too tired even to hear it. But then, she would take her phone with her wouldn't she? Anyway, schoolteachers couldn't just suddenly take off, could they?

No, it must have been something he did or said that had upset her, and she was sending him the signal that the friendship was over. What had he done though?

True, after dinner at her flat, he had left rather abruptly. He'd been very tired and his defences were low.

Dee had been particularly sweet and Dream Girl like, and he'd known that if he'd stayed, things could have got out of hand in a way, which would probably have been quite delightful, but in a way which could also have nightmare repercussions, because he still hadn't thought things through.

Now, four days later, four days that felt like four years, Jack had had plenty of time to think and he knew that the time had come for talking.

All he had to do now was find her in order to do that. He tried her cell phone again. It was still turned off.

On Friday afternoon, wild ideas about going to her flat and camping on her doorstep until she returned from school had chased each other around in his brain. But in the end, he'd worked on the radiators instead. Now he was glad because, suppose she'd turned her phone off then dropped it down a drain by mistake? He'd have looked a bit of a fool then. But, wait a minute, that must be it. Why on earth hadn't he thought of that before? Of course, that would explain the fact that she couldn't contact him — his phone number was keyed into her phone, if she'd lost her phone, she couldn't contact him.

With a relieved smile lurking at the

back of his eyes, Jack looked at his watch. Only another couple of hours to go and he would go round to Dee's, and they could have a good chat about, well, about things in general.

'You've got to pull yourself together Dee. This just isn't like you.' Gina put the last glass away in the kitchen cupboard and reached for the kettle.

Feeling very sorry for herself, Dee sat with her head in her hands. 'I will pull myself together,' she said pitifully, 'tomorrow, when my head feels better.'

'Well, it won't feel better if you don't stay off the plonk.' Gina eyed the empty wine bottle standing next to the sink. 'Honestly Dee,' if you'd wanted a bit of company last night, you know I'd have come round. To sit here all alone on a Friday night drowning your sorrows — well. We could have had a party!'

'Wasn't in a party mood. And would you lower your voice just a tad?'

The kettle boiled and a stony-faced Gina placed a mug of coffee at Dee's elbow.

'Thanks,' said Dee peering up at her through her glasses. 'And please don't you be cross with me too!'

'Why, who else is cross with you?'

'Me. I'm cross with me. I'm cross with me for having been so stupid as to fall for all this romantic nonsense about seeing a stranger in the night and falling for him before I even know him, and then being so disappointed and upset when he turns out to be a two-faced liar!'

'You and lots of others,' said Gina prosaically. 'Happens all the time. Easy mistake to make, specially bearing in mind the legs.'

Dee sniffed. 'They weren't that special.'

'That's the spirit. Now, nice shower, scrambled egg, then we'll go shopping. Shoe shopping would be excellent. We don't have to buy them, just lots of trying on!'

Dee was just about to say that no amount of shopping would ever make up for Jack turning out to be such a rat, when the doorbell rang.

'Oh no, that'll be the old biddy in the next door flat reminding me to put my cardboard out this week. Don't let her in! Tell her I'm in the shower.'

'OK,' said Gina obediently making towards the front door.

She opened the front door with her friendly to all old ladies smile on her lips — which immediately died. 'Well, hel-lo,' she said, her smile widening and the light of interest shining in her eyes. 'Let me guess, you must be Jack?'

'Right,' said a slightly puzzled looking Jack. 'Is Dee OK? Has she lost her phone? Is she all right? Perhaps she's gone to visit her parents? Anyway, who are you?'

'I thought you'd never ask,' said Gina. 'I'm Gina. You might remember me. You gatecrashed my wedding.'

'Ah, that. Well, sorry about that, but you should look after your bridesmaids better. She was standing there in her red dress . . . '

'Old Rose, actually,' interrupted Dee

from behind the sitting room door.

Jack peered past Gina into the hall. 'Are you OK Dee? I was just wondering . . . well . . . '

'She's just about to have a shower,' said Gina. 'Bit of a late Friday night, you know how it is.'

'Look, can I come in?'

'No you can't,' said Dee from behind the door.

'This is ridiculous, but rather amusing,' said Gina. She leaned back just enough to see Dee sheltering behind the sitting room door. 'He's gorgeous,' she mouthed, rolling her eyes for good measure.

'Look, just tell me what it is I'm supposed to have done,' begged Jack.

Dee stuck her head round the door.

'There you are,' said Jack with relief. 'Oh, you're wearing glasses.'

'Well done!' said Dee pushing them more firmly on to her nose. 'And I didn't say you could come in. Gina, why did you let him in?'

'Well, I didn't, he forced his way.

Anyway, I'm just going.'

'No, you're not,' said Dee clinging on to her friend's arm. 'You're not leaving me here with him.'

For a long moment Dee's indignant stare met Jack's puzzled one.

'Dee, stop playing games and just tell me what it is I'm supposed to have done.'

'Huh! I'm surprised you're out so close to Hallowe'en!'

'Eh?'

'Well, you know, with your fear of witches and all.'

'Sorry, I'm wading through treacle here. I don't quite follow.'

'No? You surprise me. I understand from Josh, you were once caught by a witch and forced to marry her. A witch who looked like a fairy princess,' she added for good measure.

The light of comprehension started in Jack's eyes. 'Oh, that witch,' murmured Gina who, despite her words, was making no attempt to leave.

Dee tightened the belt of her dressing

gown. 'I should watch the kind of bedtime stories you tell Josh. If I were you, I'd stick to Beatrix Potter. It was a story — I take it — I mean any normal person, any normal honest person, would have told me when I asked if they were married, that yes they were, or yes they had been, wouldn't they?'

'I'm divorced,' said Jack. 'And hang on a minute, I don't remember your asking me that.'

Dee turned away. 'Typical!' she said. 'You know, ever since a certain incident in my past when I was very deliberately deceived by someone, I've taken very great care to find out about people's single or marital status. So even if I didn't ask you directly, I asked you indirectly and you lied by omission. It's not the marriage I object to, it's the lie!'

Gina picked up her bag from where she'd dumped it on the hall floor. 'Yes, well, I think I will be going now. You know, things to do.' She pushed past Jack, who hardly seemed to notice her.

'So you don't even want to hear what

I have to say,' said Jack to Dee's profile.

There was a long silence.

'No, well. You never have really, have you? Right from the beginning you've always assumed I was a bad hat, up to no good, out to get you. You've always thought that just because I'm in the property game, I'm going to lie and cheat, throw little old ladies out of their homes then sell them on at a huge profit, ride roughshod over everybody's feelings but my own.'

He paused and wiped a hand across his eyes. 'I was beginning to think we might have something special here, more fool me. You don't give anyone a chance; you jump to conclusions about people and don't give them the opportunity to explain anything before taking extreme action . . . I don't need this!'

For a long moment Jack and Dee stared at one another. The air between them was charged with pent up emotions. Hardly daring to breathe, Gina pressed herself against the hall wall.

Then Jack gave a half smile. 'Shame

you're so beautiful.'

The next moment Gina and Dee were left gazing at one another in an empty hallway.

Some thirty seconds after Jack's car started, Dee burst into tears. 'It's true! Everything he said. My mother's right. I am impatient, I am extreme. I didn't give him a chance about Aunt Louisa's ashes; I didn't give him a chance over the marriage thing. I'm just an awful, awful person . . . I'm surprised I've got any friends at all!'

'Come on, Dee, don't be daft. You've got me. Well, OK, maybe not much consolation after letting a hunk like that walk out of your life, but let's try and be positive here!'

'Thanks,' said Dee on a sob. 'Thanks a lot.'

'He'll be back,' prophesied Gina. 'The amount of electricity generated between you two was enough to light up Blackpool Tower. Give him a day to recover, then go round and eat humble pie.'

'On the whole I'd rather visit the dentist for root canal treatment,' answered Dee blowing her nose.

Gina passed a clean tissue. 'I knew you'd see sense.'

11

Normally Jack liked Sundays. He always woke up early, but on a Sunday he allowed himself the luxury of an extra half hour of dozing and listening to the radio. Today however, he swung himself out of bed just as soon as the radio came on. Brook House wouldn't restore itself to its former glory alone, and once he'd committed himself to a project, Jack saw it through.

Not that certain people would believe that, thought Jack bitterly. No, certain people would believe that he, Jack, would abandon a project at the first sign of a problem. Certain people were born judgmental and would never change, would never allow anyone the benefit of the doubt.

Only problem was, Jack wasn't sure he could live without a certain person in his life judgmental or not.

Jack made himself a cup of strong tea and a bacon sandwich and decided that today was the very day to clear one of the outhouses ready for winter storage. Lots of physical exercise was exactly what he needed.

By midmorning Dee was feeling much better. Her reflection looked a trifle wan, her eyes huge in her pale face, but inside she was resolute, the time had come to apologise. It wasn't that she wanted to restart the relationship. The last thing she wanted in her life was a divorcee with a commitment problem. Far from it, she just wanted to say sorry and move on.

So she wasn't dressed up. Just jeans and a sweater; a little mascara, a little lip-gloss, and a radiant smile. Well, perhaps she couldn't quite stretch to radiant, but she'd certainly try for peaceable.

She drove very slowly towards Brook House. Her hands were shaking on the wheel and her mouth was dry. Suppose, he didn't want to see her, suppose he'd gone out the night before and found himself another girlfriend, a more understanding one? Suppose he just wasn't there?

And suppose the security gates were in place and locked? Dee stared at the gates in dismay. The one thing she hadn't reckoned on. Oh well, needs must. She put the car back in gear and continued the fifty yards to the field entrance to park and a few moments later found herself staring into the branches of the old walnut tree.

Feeling even more of a trespasser than the last time, because then at least she'd felt she had right on her side, Dee dropped as soundlessly as possible on to the soft earth on the other side of the wall. This time she chose to skirt round to the front of the house and knock on the large front door like a regular visitor, but she'd only got as far as one of the outbuildings when she heard a strange kind of yodelling.

Seconds later she realised that this was actually Jack's attempt at joining in with a soulful song about forgetting the world and laying down with, well — best not go into that.

She crept up to where the voice was coming from. It was a dusty old brick built shed which by the looks of it had half its contents spread out on the grass. There were two lawn mowers, a machine for shredding garden refuse, a rusty barbecue and a heap of bamboo canes.

'Hi,' said Dee standing nervously in the doorway, while Jack had a fight with the remaining bamboo canes.

Abruptly, the yodelling stopped. 'Hi,' answered Jack rubbing the bridge of his nose where he'd narrowly missed stabbing his eye out on the end of a cane. 'You made me jump. How did you get in?'

Dee nodded towards the wall. She'd forgotten for a moment, just how attractive Jack was. He hadn't shaved, his hair was dusty from the shed, but none of that mattered. He allowed himself a small tentative smile.

'Like some coffee?'

'Um, well. I've come to say sorry.'

'Oh?'

'Yes. Although of course, you should have told me.'

'Yes, well, I've been thinking about that. This person you mentioned who deceived you in your past? You had a relationship with him, right?'

Mutely Dee nodded.

'Hmm! And what did you say when I asked you about boyfriends? 'Boys don't make passes at girls who wear glasses' if I remember rightly? . . . And this person, this past boyfriend, I suppose you never got past the hand holding stage with him did you?'

Dee's face by now was a fiery red. 'I know, I'm sorry.'

'So you won't tolerate a 'lie by omission', from me, but it's OK for you to distort the facts a little, and make up the odd six foot two boyfriend? That's allowed?'

'I've said I'm sorry. I didn't come in order to argue. I'll go now,' said Dee turning away.

A strong hand landed on her shoulder. 'No, don't go,' said Jack. 'There are things I want to say, to explain about. I didn't tell you I was once married because I was scared it would put you off. I made a mistake, a big mistake. We were too young. She wanted the wedding day, I wanted the marriage. After the wedding day she wanted to continue a single life. I didn't.'

There was a pause in which Dee could hear the radio DJ prattling on about classic melodies from the past.

'I will never,' went on Jack, 'marry again — unless I'm sure that the word marriage is fully understood by both partners. By and large I don't explain this to people, especially not on a first date, it's a bit heavy if you know what I mean . . .

'I'm not up for casual relationships, if I feel myself getting too involved I back off fast, and I'm only telling you this because, well I fell for you like a ton of bricks first time we met. And I didn't trust it. I can't rush these things, even when it feels so right. I just can't . . . I'm sorry, but that's how it is. I have to have time.'

Dee turned to face him. 'It's all right, Jack, I understand. I've got my hang ups too. I truly only came to say I'm sorry,' she looked away from Jack and towards the house which stood bathed in the mellow autumn sunshine. 'And whatever you decide to do with Brook House I hope it goes well for you.'

She was looking back now, straight into Jack's eyes.

He blinked. 'Oh, don't!'

'Don't what?'

'Don't give me that Bambi look!'

'What d'you mean — Bambi look?' asked Dee, her eyes still fixed unwaveringly on his.

In the background she could hear the DJ announcing the next song. 'Here's one for the romantic among you,' he said. 'It's all about a lady who's wearing a red dress.'

Jack stared at her intently, the

crooked smile on his lips belying the seriousness of his eyes. 'Dance with me!'

Wordlessly she moved into his arms, and on the rough uncut lawn of Brook House, surrounded by old lawn mowers and other rusty paraphernalia, Dee and Jack started on the first dance of the rest of their lives together.

THE END

We do hope that you have enjoyed reading this large print book.

Did you know that all of our titles are available for purchase?

We publish a wide range of high quality large print books including:
Romances, Mysteries, Classics
General Fiction
Non Fiction and Westerns

Special interest titles available in large print are:
The Little Oxford Dictionary
Music Book, Song Book
Hymn Book, Service Book

Also available from us courtesy of Oxford University Press:
Young Readers' Dictionary
(large print edition)
Young Readers' Thesaurus
(large print edition)

For further information or a free brochure, please contact us at:
Ulverscroft Large Print Books Ltd.,
The Green, Bradgate Road, Anstey,
Leicester, LE7 7FU, England.
Tel: (00 44) **0116 236 4325**
Fax: (00 44) **0116 234 0205**

NO MISTAKING LOVE

Moyra Tarling

Working at Moonbeam Lake, it wasn't easy for single mother Laura Matthews. She wanted her twins to enjoy summer in the place she'd once loved — despite its painful memories. But she hadn't counted on Tanner Mcleod's reappearance. Six years ago, she'd comforted him when his brother died, and it had led to passion. But Tanner had left before she'd discovered the consequences of their love. How could she confess that *he* was the father the twins had never met?

KNAVE OF DIAMONDS

Wendy Kremer

Sharon is employed by a retailer to write some PR text about Patrick, a famous jewellery designer, who's creating an exclusive collection for the everyday woman. Patrick's initial resentment of Sharon changes when he gets to know her, whilst she admits that he's a fascinating man. If only other women didn't think so too! Then as Sharon and Patrick visit Hong Kong for a photo session things begin to buzz — only to fall apart. What has fate designed for them?

TAKE A CHANCE ON LOVE

Claire Dalton

After returning to her home town, Catherine Earnshaw plans to spend all her time on her job at the local newspaper and caring for her elderly father. One thing she's sure of is that there's no room for a man in her new life. She's been hurt once before and she daren't allow herself to fall for the enigmatic Sean Bradford-Jones, or rely on him when all her plans start to unravel . . .

THE TREASURE SEEKERS

Anne Holman

Not comfortable with the genteel life of a spinster in Bath, Frances longs to go and find her father, Professor Arthur Cannon, presumed missing whilst on a plant-hunting mission in Central America. To her mother's dismay Frances happily joins her aunt and uncle on an expedition to the Gulf of Mexico. On the way she meets the intriguing, but secretive, George Webster. Her adventures begin, but will she find her father — and can she also find love?

A MATTER OF PRIDE

Margaret Mounsdon

Working for the opera star Bede Evans and his glamorous wife Jasmine is the perfect job for Rhianna O'Neill — until she inherits a wilful sixteen-year-old half sister after the tragic death of their mother in an accident . . . Then Rhianna's life is shattered by her broken engagement to Sax, Bede and Jasmine's son, and she takes off for France with handsome Luc Fermier, an old flame from her past. But that is when her problems really begin . . .

PLACE OF HEALING

Paula Williams

When talented cook Jess is betrayed
by her boyfriend and best friend,
she has to get away, so she books a
holiday cottage in a remote corner
of Somerset. And Higher Neston
immediately feels like home, her
landlady Elsie like family. Jess lacks
confidence in her own instincts, yet
finding herself caught in the middle
of family quarrels and old rivalries,
she must learn to listen to her heart
and decide who is trustworthy . . .